Hugo 1942

# A Spy in the House of Love

# A Spy in the House of Love

## Anaïs Nin

SWALLOW PRESS
ATHENS

Printed in the United States of America
02 01 00 97 96 95   10 9 8 7 6

Swallow Press and Ohio University Press books are printed on acid-free paper ∞


Library of Congress Cataloging-in-Publication Data

Nin, Anaïs, 1903-1977
    A spy in the house of love

    I. Title
    PS3527.I865S6     1984     813'52 83-24188
    ISBN 0-8040-0280-0

# Foreword

Anaïs Nin's *Diary* is generally recognized today as her major, in fact monumental contribution to twentieth-century literature, a unique record of a woman's self-creation. But for many years, until late in her life, its publication, even selectively, had been impossible. Aside from the practical problems of commercial publishing, of censorship and the all-pervading puritanical climate of the times, Anaïs Nin had been reluctant and fearful to expose herself, her husband, her family, her friends and lovers, to the intimate revelations secreted in its more than 35,000 pages. Initiated in 1914, when she was eleven years old, to cope with the traumatic loss of her father who had deserted the family for another woman, and with the circumstances of her first, involuntary exile in America, the diary had provided a lifelong confidant and confessor. Here she recorded and examined, often in painful and frank detail, the "high moments" of her life. It contained the "truth" of her confrontations with emotional problems, with sex and love, with her insatiable need for extraordinary adventures. It mirrored her fragmentation and the guilt feelings arising from her pursuit of sexual freedom and unattainable satisfaction.

As a writer who believed that experience rather than invention provided the bedrock for any artistic creation, but who could not reveal during her lifetime the true record of her own experiences, Anaïs Nin was forced to transpose and transmute essential diary material into fiction. "What is it allotted me to say?" she had proclaimed in her very first work of fiction, the "prose-poem" *The House of Incest,* in 1936. "Only the truth disguised as a fairy tale." Her novels and stories, she often confessed, were merely the "outcroppings," the artistic "distillations" of her intimate, secret diaries.

*A Spy in the House of Love,* published first in 1954 and eventually incorporated as the fourth volume in her *roman fleuve, Cities of the Interior,* is perhaps one of the most accomplished, most effective of these distillations. It emerged at a time when Anaïs Nin's

1

personal life was riven once again by conflicting loyalties. The irresistible pull of a new love relationship developing in California was taking her away from her husband's world in New York, and she was laying the foundations for the bi-coastal life she would pursue, in conspiratorial secrecy, until her death in Los Angeles early in 1977.

"It was when she saw the lives of spies," Sabina, the central character in these pages, observes, "that she realized fully the tension with which she lived every moment. . . . The fear of committing themselves, of sleeping too soundly, of talking in their sleep, of carelessness. The need for continued pretending, quick improvisations, quick justifications of their presence here and there."

When Anaïs Nin, in her essay volume *The Novel of the Future,* in 1968, discussed the various elements that went into the writing of *A Spy in the House of Love,* she obviously did not want to touch upon the very personal relevance of the story as a reflection of her own emotional dilemmas. "I see Sabina as a portrait of modern woman," she noted, "seeking to break taboos, but still a prey to guilt." Yet the personal element, the "truth" underlying her artistic distillation, the sources of her creation, are always evident, especially to the readers of the more recently published unexpurgated volumes of her *Diary.*

"Was it Sabina now rushing into her ritual of pleasure," Anaïs Nin writes in *A Spy in the House of Love,* "or was it her father within her, his blood guiding her amorousness, dictating her intrigues. She could never know which one was Sabina, which one her father whose role she had assumed by alchemy of mimetic love."

Having read Dr. Otto Rank's *Don Juan et le Double* in 1932, she had taken up his point that there are "more complex motivations behind sensual restlessness" than the usual, simplistic portrayals of this age-old figure. The complex female equivalent she had created in Sabina, obviously, was meant to transcend the stereotypical image of the nymphomaniac which she, herself, had found so diminishing and objectionable. "I meant to picture a woman's struggle to liberate herself sexually from connecting the sex and

2

love," she told an interviewer in Europe in 1966.

Anaïs Nin's relentless self-analysis, of course, was a driving force behind her diary writing and her ongoing attempts to discover and articulate her self artistically. Painfully aware of her deeply divided self, of social restrictions and self-created inhibitions, she asked, time and again, whether it would be possible "to live out each different part of the self simultaneously" without devastating consequences. Could one, as Sabina tried to do so desperately, indulge one's sensual restlessness, one's fancies and imaginings as a woman, and still remain in love and loyal to the man one was married to?

"She was tired of pulling these disparate fragments together," Anaïs Nin's voice seems to mingle with that of her character, Sabina. "It was perhaps at such moments of isolation that Madame Bovary had taken the poison. It was the moment when the hidden life is in danger of being exposed, and no woman could bear the condemnation. But why should she fear exposure? Was it merely this figure of the lie detector dogging her steps which caused her so acute an anxiety?

"Guilt is the one burden human beings cannot bear alone.

"She needed a confessor! Would she find it there, in the world of the artists?"

Anaïs Nin, the lapsed Catholic who once had wanted to become a saint, had found her confessor already in the endless pages of her diary. With *A Spy in the House of Love* she had, once again, found a way to unburden herself in public, as it were, transporting her confession into "the world of the artists."

In her story, as in her life, Anaïs Nin persistently hoped that living out a fragmented, divided self did not need to end in tragedy and dispersion. "I felt there could be another end," she had explained while recalling the genesis of *A Spy in the House of Love*. "It need not end in madness. It can cause a shock of awareness. As in all divided selves, Sabina lives in relationships which are partly imagined. Both the unreality of them and of her whole life, besides

3

a feeling of dispersion and fragmentation, made her wish for someone who could follow the erratic course of her acts, synthesize her, even if it meant doing so within the context of guilt and judgement."

However, in the end, there seems to be no savior who would synthesize Sabina, make her whole; there is no redemption, no absolution, just as there is no resolution, no end, to the ongoing flow of Anaïs Nin's diary. There is, merely, the act of confession contained in the veiled revelations of the story itself and a glimpse of what might yet happen to its troubled protagonist:

> "Free me," said Sabina to the lie detector. "Set me free. I've said this to so many men. . . ."
> "You have to set yourself free. That will come with love. . . ."
> "Oh, I've loved enough, if that could save one."
> "You haven't loved yet," he said. "You've only been trying to love, beginning to love."

When Anaïs Nin concluded *A Spy in the House of Love* she seemed to have been cautiously optimistic that in spite of her own sense of guilt and her apprehension of society's judgement concerning her own life, reflected in the fictional Sabina, she would find the elusive "whole woman" she had been searching for all her life. But along the way she had also written in these pages that "every spy's life had ended in ignominious death."

*Becket, Massachusetts, Summer 1995*          *Gunther Stuhlmann*

The lie detector was asleep when he heard the telephone ringing.

At first he believed it was the clock ordering him to rise, but then he awakened completely and remembered his profession.

The voice he heard was rusty, as if disguised. He could not distinguish what altered it: alcohol, drugs, anxiety or fear.

It was a woman's voice; but it could have been an adolescent imitating a woman, or a woman imitating an adolescent.

"What is it?" he asked. "Hello. Hello. Hello."

"I had to talk to someone; I can't sleep. I had to call someone."

"You have something to confess . . ."

"To confess?" echoed the voice incredulously; this time, the ascending tonalities unmistakably feminine.

"Don't you know who I am?"

"No, I just dialed blindly. I've done this before. It is good to hear a voice in the middle of the night, that's all."

"Why a stranger? You could call a friend."

"A stranger doesn't ask questions."

"But it's my profession to ask questions."

"Who are you?"

"A lie detector."

There was a long silence after his words. The lie detector expected her to hang up. But he heard her cough through the telephone.

"Are you there?"

"Yes."

"I thought you would hang up."

There was laughter through the telephone, a lax, spangled, spiralling laughter. "But you don't practice your profession over the telephone!"

"It's true. Yet you wouldn't have called me if you were innocent. Guilt is the one burden human beings can't bear alone. As soon as a crime is committed, there is a telephone call, or a confession to strangers."

"There was no crime."

"There is only one relief: to confess, to be caught, tried, punished. That's the ideal of every criminal. But it's not quite so simple. Only half of the self wants to atone, to be freed of the torments of guilt. The other half of man wants to continue to be free. So only half of the self surrenders, calling out "catch me," while the other half creates obstacles, difficulties; seeks to escape. It's a flirtation with justice. If justice is nimble, it will follow the clue with the criminal's help. If not, the criminal will take care of his own atonement."

"Is that worse?"

"I think so. I think we are more severe judges of our own acts than professional judges. We judge our thoughts, our intents, our secret curses, our secret hates, not only our acts."

She hung up.

The lie detector called up the operator, gave orders to have the call traced. It came from a bar. Half an hour later, he was sitting there.

He did not allow his eyes to roam or examine. He wanted his ears alone to be attentive, that he might recognize the voice.

When she ordered a drink, he lifted his eyes from his newspaper.

Dressed in red and silver, she evoked the sounds and imagery of fire engines as they tore through the streets of New York, alarming the heart with the violent gong of catastrophe; all dressed in red and silver, the tearing red and silver cutting a pathway through the flesh. The first time he looked at her he felt: *everything will burn!*

Out of the red and silver and the long cry of alarm to the poet who survives in all human beings, as the child survives in him; to this poet she threw an unexpected ladder in the middle of the city and ordained, "Climb!"

As she appeared, the orderly alignment of the city gave way before this ladder one was invited to climb, standing straight in space like the ladder of Baron Munchausen which led to the sky.

Only her ladder led to fire.

He looked at her again with a professional frown.

She could not sit still. She talked profusely and continuously with a feverish breathlessness like one in fear of silence. She sat as if she could not bear to sit for long; and, when she rose to buy cigarettes, she was equally eager to return to her seat. Impatient, alert, watchful, as if in dread of being attacked, restless and keen, she drank hurriedly; she smiled so swiftly that he was not even certain it had been a smile; she listened only partially to what was being said to her; and, even when someone in the bar leaned over and shouted a name in her direction, she did not respond at first, as if it were not her own.

"Sabina!" shouted the man from the bar, leaning towards her perilously but not losing his grip on the back of his chair for fear of toppling.

Someone nearer to her gallantly repeated the name for her, which she finally acknowledged as her own. At this moment, the lie detector threw off the iridescence which the night, the voice, the drug of sleep and her presence had created in him, and determined that she behaved like someone who had all the symptoms of guilt: her way of looking at the door of the bar, as if expecting the proper moment to make her escape; her unpremeditated talk, without continuity; her erratic and sudden gestures, unrelated to her talk; the chaos of her phrases; her sudden, sulky silences.

As friends drifted towards her, sat with her, and then drifted away to other tables, she was forced to raise her voice, usually low, to be heard above the cajoling blues.

She was talking about a party at which indistinct incidents had taken place, hazy scenes from which the lie detector could not distinguish the heroine or the victim; talking a broken dream, with spaces, reversals, retractions, and galloping fantasies. She was now in Morocco visiting the baths with the native women, sharing their pumice stone, and learning from the prostitutes how to paint her eyes with kohl from the market place. "It's coal dust, and you place it right inside the eyes. It smarts at first, and you want to cry; but that spreads it out on the eyelids, and that is how they get that shiny, coal black rim around the eyes."

"Didn't you get an infection?" asked someone at her right whom the lie detector could not see clearly, an indistinct personage she disregarded even as she answered, "Oh, no, the prostitutes have the kohl blessed at the mosque." And then, when everyone laughed at this which she did not consider humorous, she laughed with them; and now it was as if all she had said had been written on a huge blackboard, and she took a sponge and effaced it all by a phrase which left in suspense who had been at the baths; or, perhaps, this was a story she had read, or heard at a bar; and, as soon as it was erased in the mind of her listeners, she began another . . .

The faces and the figures of her personages appeared only half drawn; and, when the lie detector had just begun to perceive them, another face and figure were interposed as in a dream. And, when he believed she had been talking about a woman, it turned out that it was not a woman, but a man; and, when the image of the man began to form, it turned out the lie detector had not heard aright: it was a young man who resembled a woman who had once taken care of Sabina; and this young man was instantly metamorphosed into a group of people who had humiliated her one night.

He could not retain a sequence of the people she had loved, hated, escaped from, any more than he could keep track of the changes in her personal appearance by phrases such as, "at that time my hair was blond," "at that time I was married," and who it was that had been forgotten or betrayed; and, when in desperation he clung to the recurrences of certain words, they formed no design by their repetition, but rather an absolute contradiction. The word, "actress," recurred most persistently; and yet the lie detector could not, after hours of detection, tell whether she was an actress, or wanted to be one, or was pretending.

She was compelled by a confessional fever which forced her into lifting a corner of the veil, and then frightened when anyone listened too attentively. She repeatedly took a giant sponge and erased all she had said by absolute denial, as if this confusion were in itself a mantle of protection.

At first she beckoned and lured one into her world; then, she blurred the passageways, confused all the images, as if to elude detection.

The dawn appearing at the door silenced her. She tightened her cape around her shoulders as if it were the final threat, the greatest enemy of all. To the dawn she would not even address a feverish speech. She stared at it angrily, and left the bar.

The lie detector followed her.

Before she awakened Sabina's dark eyes showed the hard light of precious stones through a slit in the eyelids, pure dark green beryl shining, not yet warmed by her feverishness.

Then instantly she was awake, on guard.

She did not awaken gradually, in abandon and trust to the new day. As soon as light or sound registered on her consciousness, danger was in the air and she sat up to meet its thrusts.

Her first expression was one of tension, which was not beauty. Just as anxiety dispersed the strength of the body, it also gave to the face a wavering, tremulous vagueness, which was not beauty, like that of a drawing out of focus.

Slowly what she composed with the new day was her own focus, to bring together body and mind. This was made with an effort, as if all the dissolutions and dispersions of her self the night before were difficult to reassemble. She was like an actress who must compose a face, an attitude to meet the day.

The eyebrow pencil was no mere charcoal emphasis on blond eyebrows, but a design necessary to balance a chaotic asymmetry. Make up and powder were not simply applied to heighten a porcelain texture, to efface the uneven swellings caused by sleep, but to smooth out the sharp furroughs designed by nightmares, to reform the contours and blurred surfaces of the cheeks, to erase the contradictions and conflicts which strained the clarity of the face's lines, disturbing the purity of its forms.

She must redesign the face, smooth the anxious brows, separate the crushed eyelashes, wash off the traces of secret interior tears, accentuate the mouth as upon a

11

canvas, so it will hold its luxuriant smile.

Inner chaos, like those secret volcanoes which suddenly lift the neat furrows of a peacefully ploughed field, awaited behind all disorders of face, hair and costume, for a fissure through which to explode.

What she saw in the mirror now was a flushed, clear-eyed face, smiling, smooth, beautiful. The multiple acts of composure and artifice had merely dissolved her anxieties; now that she felt prepared to meet the day, her true beauty emerged which had been frayed and marred by anxiety.

She considered her clothes with the same weighing of possible external dangers as she had the new day which had entered through her closed windows and doors.

Believing in the danger which sprang from objects as well as people, which dress, which shoes, which coat demanded less of her panicked heart and body? For a costume was a challenge too, a discipline, a trap which once adopted could influence the actor.

She ended by choosing a dress with a hole in its sleeve. The last time she had worn it, she had stood before a restaurant which was too luxurious, too ostentatious, which she was frightened to enter, but instead of saying: "I am afraid to enter here," she had been able to say: "I can't enter here with a hole in my sleeve."

She selected her cape which seemed more protective, more enveloping.

Also the cape held within its folds something of what she imagined was a quality possessed exclusively by man: some dash, some audacity, some swagger of freedom denied to woman.

The toreador's provocative flings, the medieval horse-men's floating flag of attack, a sail unfurled in full collision with the wind, the warrior's shield for his face in battle, all these she experienced when she placed a cape around her shoulder.

A spread out cape was the bed of nomads, a cape unfurled was the flag of adventure.

Now she was dressed in a costume most appropriate to flights, battles, tournaments.

The curtain of the night's defencelessness was rising to expose a personage prepared.

Prepared, said the mirror, prepared said the shoes, prepared said the cape.

She stood contemplating herself arrayed for no peaceful or trusting encounter with life.

She was not surprised when she looked out of her window and saw the man who had been following her standing at the corner pretending to be reading a newspaper.

It was not a surprise, because it was a materialization of a feeling she had known for many years: that of an Eye watching and following her throughout her life.

She walked along 18th St. towards the river. She walked slightly out of rhythm, like someone not breathing deeply, long steps and inclined forward as if racing.

It was a street completely lined with truck garages. At this hour they were sliding open the heavy iron doors and huge trucks were rolling out, obscuring the sun. Their wheels were as tall as Sabina.

They lined up so close together that she could no longer see the street or the houses across the way. On her right they made a wall of throbbing motors, and giant wheels starting to turn. On her left more doors were opening, more trucks advanced slowly as if to engulf her. They loomed threateningly, inhuman, so high she could not see the drivers.

Sabina felt a shrinking of her whole body, and as she shrank from the noise, the trucks seem to enlarge in her eyes, their scale becoming monstrous, the rolling of their wheels uncontrollable. She felt as a child in an enormous world of menacing giants. She felt her bones fragile in her sandals. She felt brittle and crushable. She felt overwhelmed by danger, by a mechanized evil.

Her feeling of fragility was so strong that she was startled by the appearance of a woman at her left, who walked in step with her. Sabina glanced at her profile and was comforted by her tallness, the assurance of her walk. She too was dressed in black, but walked without terror.

And then she vanished. The mirror had come to an end. Sabina had been confronted with herself, the life size image walking beside the shrunk inner self, proving to her once more the disproportion between her feelings and external truth.

As many other times Sabina had experienced small-ness, a sense of gigantic dangers, but she faced in the mirror a tall, strong, mature woman of thirty, equal to her surroundings. In the mirror was the image of what she had become and the image she gave to the world, but her secret inner self could be overwhelmed by a large truck wheel.

It was always at this precise moment of diminished power, that the image of her husband Alan appeared. It required a mood of weakness in her, some inner un-balance, some exaggeration in her fears, to summon the image of Alan. He appeared as a fixed point in space. A calm face. A calm bearing. A tallness which made him visible in crowds, and which harmonized with her concept of his uniqueness. The image of Alan appeared in her vision like a snap-shot. It did not reach her through tactile memory, or any of the senses but the eyes. She did not remember his touch, or his voice. He was a photograph in her mind, with the static pose which characterized him: either standing up above average tallness so that he must carry his head a little bent, and something calm which gave the impression of a kind of benediction. She could not see him playful, smiling, or reckless, or carefree. He would never speak first, assert his mood, likes or dislikes, but wait, as confessors do, to catch first of all the words or the moods of others. It gave him the passive quality of a listener, a reflector. She could not imagine him wanting anything badly (except that she should come home) or taking anything for himself. In the two snap-shots she carried he showed two facets but no contrasts: one listen-

15

ing and waiting, wise, and detached, the other sitting in meditation as a spectator.

Whatever event (in this case the trivial one of the walk down 18th. St.) caused in Sabina either a panic, a shrinking, these two images of Alan would appear, and her desire to return home.

She walked back to the room in which she had awakened that morning. She pulled her valise out from under the bed and began to pack it.

The cashier at the desk of the Hotel smiled at her as she passed, on her way out, a smile which appeared to Sabina as expressing a question, a doubt. The man at the desk stared at her valise. Sabina walked up to the desk and said haltingly: "Didn't . . . my husband pay the bill?"

"Your husband took care of everything," said the desk man.

Sabina flushed angrily. She was about to say: Then why did you stare at me? And why the undertone of irony in your faces? And why had she herself hesitated at the word husband?

The mockery of the hotel personnel added to her mood of weight and fatigue. Her valise seem to grow heavier in her hand. In this mood of lostness every object became extraordinarily heavy, every room oppressive, every task overwhelming. Above all, the world seemed filled with condemning eyes. The cashier's smile had been ironic and the desk man's scrutiny not friendly.

Haven was only two blocks away, yet distance seemed enormous, difficulties insuperable. She stopped a taxi and said: "55 Fifth Avenue."

The taxi driver said rebelliously: "Why, lady, that's

only two blocks away, you can walk it. You look strong enough." And he sped away.

She walked slowly. The house she reached was luxurious, but as many houses in the village, without elevators. There was no one around to carry her bag. The two floors she had to climb appeared like the endless stairways in a nightmare. They would drain the very last of her strength. *But I am safe. He will be asleep. He will be happy at my coming. He will be there. He will open his arms. He will make room for me. I will no longer have to struggle.*

Just before she reached the last floor she could see a thin ray of light under his door and she felt a warm joy permeate her entire body. *He is there. He is awake.*

As if everything else she had experienced were but ordeals and this the shelter, the place of happiness.

*I can't understand what impels me to leave this, this is happiness.*

When his door opened it always seems to open upon an unchanging room. The furniture was never displaced, the lights were always diffused and gentle like sanctuary lamps.

Alan stood at the door and what she saw first of all was his smile. He had strong, very even teeth in a long and narrow head. The smile almost closed his eyes which were narrow and shed a soft fawn light. He stood very erect with an almost military bearing, and being very tall his head bent down as if from its own weight to look down upon Sabina.

He always greeted her with a tenderness which seemed to assume she had always been in great trouble. He automatically rushed to comfort and to shelter. The way he

17

opened his arms and the tone in which he greeted her implied: "First of all I will comfort and console you, first of all I will gather you together again, you're always so battered by the world outside."

The strange, continuous, almost painful tension she felt away from him always dissolved in his presence, at his very door.

He took her valise, moving with deliberate gestures, and deposited with care in her closet. There was a rock-like center to his movements, a sense of perfect gravitation. His emotions, his thoughts revolved around a fixed center like a well organized planetary system.

The trust she felt in his evenly modulated voice, both warm and light, in his harmonious manners never sudden or violent, in his thoughts which he weighed before articulating, in his insights which were moderate, was so great that it resembled a total abandon of herself to him, a total giving.

In trust she flowed out to him, grateful and warm.

She placed him apart from other men, distinct and unique. He held the only fixed position in the fluctuations of her feelings.

"Tired my little one?" he said. "Was it a hard trip? Was it a success?"

He was only five years older than she was. He was thirty five and had gray hairs on his temples, and he talked to her as if he were her father. Had he always talked in this tone to her? She tried to remember Alan as a very young man. When she was twenty years old and he twenty-five. But she could not picture him any differently than at this moment. At twenty-five he stood the same way, he spoke the same way, and even then he said: "My little one."

For a moment, because of the caressing voice, the acceptance and the love he showed, she was tempted to say: "Alan, I am not an actress, I was not playing a part on the road, I never left New York, it was all an invention. I stayed in a hotel, with . . ."

She held her breath. That was what she was always doing, holding her breath so that the truth would never come out, at any time, not here with Alan, and not in the hotel room with a lover, who had asked questions about Alan. She held her breath to choke the truth, made one more effort to be the very actress she denied being, to act the part she denied acting, to describe this trip she had not taken, to recreate the woman who had been away for eight days, so that the smile would not vanish from Alan's face, so that his trustingness and happiness would not be shattered.

During the brief suspense of her breathing she was able to make the transition. It was an actress who stood before Alan now, re-enacting the past eight days.

"The trip was tiring, but the play went well. I hated the role at first, as you know. But I began to feel for Madame Bovary, and the second night I played it well, I even understood her particular kind of voice and gestures. I changed myself completely. You know, how tension makes the voice higher and thinner, and nervousness increases the number of gestures?"

"What an actress you are," said Alan, "you're still doing it! You've entered into this woman's part so thoroughly you can't get out of it! You're actually making

19

so many more gestures than you ever did, and your voice has changed. Why do you keep covering your mouth with your hand? As if you were holding back something you were strongly tempted to say?"

"Yes, that is what *she* was doing. I must stop. I'm so tired, so tired, and I can't stop . . . can't stop being her."

"I want my own Sabina back."

Because Alan had said this was a part she had been playing, because he had said this was not Sabina, not the genuine one, the one he loved, Sabina began to feel that the woman who had been away eight days, who had stayed at a small hotel with a lover, who had been disturbed by the unstability of that other relationship, the strangeness of it, into a mounting anxiety expressed in multiple movements, wasted, unnecessary, like the tumult of wind or water, was indeed another woman, a part she had played on the road. The valise, the impermanency, the evanescent quality of the eight days were thus explained. Nothing that had happened had any connection with Sabina herself, only with her profession. She had returned home intact, able to answer his loyalty with loyalty, his trust with trust, his single love with a single love.

"I want my own Sabina back, not this woman with a new strange gesture she had never made before, of covering her face, her mouth with her hand as if she were about to say something she did not want to say or should not say."

He asked more questions. And now that she was moving away from the description of the role she had played into descriptions of a town, a hotel, and other people in the cast, she felt this secret, this anguishing constriction tightening her heart, an invisible flush of shame, invisible to others but burning in her like a fever. It was this shame which dressed her suddenly, permeated her gestures, clouded her beauty, her eyes with a sudden opaqueness. She experienced it as a loss of beauty, an absence of quality.

Every improvisation, every invention to Alan was always followed not by any direct knowledge of this shame, but by a substitution: almost as soon as she had talked, she felt as if her dress had faded, her eyes dimmed, she felt unlovely, unlovable, not beautiful enough, not of a quality deserving to be loved.

*Why am I loved by him? Will he continue to love me? His love is for something I am not. I am not beautiful enough, I am not good, I am not good for him, he should not love me, I do not deserve it, shame shame shame for not being beautiful enough, there are other women so much more beautiful, with radiant faces and clear eyes. Alan says my eyes are beautiful, but I cannot see them, to me they are lying eyes, my mouth lies, only a few hours ago it was kissed by another ... He is kissing the mouth kissed by another, he is kissing eyes which adored another ... shame ... shame ... shame ... the lies, the lies ... The clothes he is hanging up for me with such care were caressed and crushed by another, the other was so impatient he crushed and tore at my dress. I had no time to undress. It is this dress he is hanging up lovingly ... can I forget yesterday, forget the vertigo, this wildness, can I come home and stay home? Sometimes I cannot bear the quick changes of scene, the quick transitions,*

21

*I cannot make the changes smoothly, from one relation-
ship to another. Some parts of me tear off like a fragment,
fly here and there. I lose vital parts of myself, some part
of me stays in that hotel room, a part of me is walking
away from this place of haven, a part of me is following
another as he walks down the street alone, or perhaps not
alone: someone may take my place at his side while I am
here, that will be my punishment, and someone will take
my place here when I leave. I feel guilty for leaving each
one alone, I feel responsible for their being alone, and I
feel guilty twice over, towards both men. Wherever I am,
I am in many pieces, not daring to bring them all together, anymore than I would dare to bring the two men
together. Now I am here where I will not be hurt, for a
few days at least I will not be hurt in any way, by any
word or gesture . . . but I am not all of me here, only half
of me is being sheltered. Well, Sabina, you failed as an
actress. You rejected the discipline, the routine, the
monotony, the repetitions, any sustained effort, and now
you have a role which must be changed every day, to
protect one human being from sorrow. Wash your lying
eyes and lying face, wear the clothes which stayed in the
house, which are his, baptized by his hands, play the role
of a whole woman, at least you have always wished to be
that, it is not altogether a lie . . .*

Alan never understood her eagerness to take a bath, her
immediate need to change her clothes, to wash off the
old make up.

The pain of dislocation and division abated, the shame
dissolved as Sabina passed into Alan's mood of content-
ment.

At this moment she feels impelled by a force outside of herself to be the woman he demands, desires, and creates. Whatever he says of her, about her, she will fulfill. She no longer feels responsibility for what she has been. There is a modification of her face and body, of her attitudes and her voice. She has become the woman Alan loves.

The feelings which flow through her and which carry her along, are of love, protection, devotion. These feelings create a powerful current on which she floats. Because of their strength they have engulfed all her doubts, as in the case of fanatic devotions to a country, a science, an art, when all minor crimes are absolved by the unquestioned value of the aim.

A light like a small diamond facet appeared in her eyes, fixed in a narrower precision on her intent. At other times her pupils were dilated, and did not seem to focus on the present, but now their diamond precision was at work on this laborious weaving of life-giving lies, and it gave them a clarity which was even more transparent than that of truth.

Sabina wants to be the woman whom Alan wants her to be.

At times Alan is not certain of what he wishes. Then the stormy, tumultuous Sabina waits in incredible stillness, alert and watchful for signs of his wishes and fantasies.

The new self she offered him, created for him, appeared intensely innocent, newer than any young girl could have been, because it was like a pure abstraction of a woman, an idealized figure, not born of what she was,

23

but of his wish and hers. She even altered her rhythm for him, surrendered her heavy restless gestures, her liking for large objects, large rooms, for timelessness, for caprice and sudden actions. Even her hands which were sturdy, for his sake rested more gently upon objects around her.

"You always wanted to be an actress, Sabina. It makes me happy that you're fulfilling this wish. It consoles me for your absences."

For his pleasure she began to reconstruct the events of the last week of her absence: the trip to Provincetown, the behaviour of the cast, the problems in the play directing errors, the reactions of the public, the night when the fuses burnt out, the night when the sound track broke down.

At the same time she wished she could tell him what had actually happened; she wished she could rest her head upon his shoulder as upon a protective force, a protective understanding not concerned with possession of her but a complete knowledge of her which would include absolution. Wishing he might judge her acts with. the same detachment and wisdom he applied to other's acts, wishing he might absolve her as he absolved strangers from a knowledge of their motivations.

Above all she wished for his *absolution* so that she might sleep deeply. She knew what awaited her instead of sleep: an anxious watch in the night. For after she had reconstructed the events of the last week for Alan's peace of mind, after he had kissed her with gratitude, and with a hunger accumulated during her absence, he fell into a deep sleep in utter abandon and confidence in the night which had brought Sabina back, while Sabina lay awake wondering whether among her inventions there might be one which could be exposed later, wondering whether her description of the Provincetown hotel might be proved false, being based on hearsay. Wondering whether she would remember what she had said about it, and what she had said about the other members of the cast. Wondering if Alan might meet one of the actors in the cast some day and discover Sabina had never worked with them at all.

The night came merely as a dark stage upon which invented scenes took on a greater sharpness than by day. Scenes surrounded by darkness were like the scenes in a dream, heightened, delineated intensely, and all the while suggesting the abysses surrounding the circles of light.

Outside of this room, this bed, there was a black precipice. She had escaped danger for a day, that was all. Other dangers awaited her to-morrow.

At night too, she puzzled the mystery of her desperate need of kindness. As other girls prayed for handsomeness in a lover, or for wealth, or for power, or for poetry, she had prayed fervently: let him be kind.

Why should she have had such a need of kindness? Was she a cripple? What if instead she had married a man of violence, or a man of cruelty?

At the mere word: cruelty, her heart started to beat feverishly. The enormity of the dangers she had averted ..as so great she did not even dare picture them. She had desired and obtained kindness. And now that she had found it she risked its loss every day, every hour, on other quests!

Alan slept so peacefully. Even in sleep he maintained

a serenity of gestures. The firm design of his nose, mouth and chin, the angular lines of the body, all sculptured from some material of rectitude that would not slacken. In moments of desire even, he did not have the wildness of the eyes, disordered hair of others. He would never grow almost delirious with pleasure, or utter sounds not quite human, from the jungle of man's earlier animalism. Was it this quietism that inspired her trust? He told no lies. What he felt and thought he could tell Sabina. At the thought of confession, of confiding in him, she was almost asleep when out of the darkness the image of Alan appeared vividly and he was sobbing, sobbing desperately as he had at his father's death. This image wakened her with horror, with compassion, and again her feeling was: I must always be on guard, to protect his happiness, always on guard to protect my guardian angel . . .

In the darkness she relived entirely the eight days spent in Provincetown.

She had walked into the dunes in quest of O'Neil's house, and had lost her way. The sand dunes were so white in the sun, so immaculate, that she felt like the first inhabitant at the top of a glacier.

The sea churned at the base as if struggling to drag back the sand into its depths, carrying a little away each time only to replace it at high tide in the form of geological designs, a static sea of crystallized sand waves.

There she stopped and took off her bathing suit to lie in the sun. Drifts of sand were lifted by the wind and deposited over her skin like muslin. She wondered whether if she stayed there long enough it would cover her, and would she disappear in a natural tomb. Immobility always brought this image to her, the image of death, and it was this which impelled her to rise and seek activity. Repose, to her, resembled death.

But here in this moment of warmth and light with her face towards the sky, the sea coiling and uncoiling violently at her feet, she did not fear the image of death. She lay still watching the wind forming sand drawings, and felt a momentary suspense from anxiety and fever. Happiness had been defined once as the absence of fever. Then what was it she possessed which was the opposite of fever?

She was grateful that hypnotized by the sun's reassuring splendor and the sea's incurable restlessness, her own nerves did not coil and spring within her to destroy this moment of repose.

It was at this moment that she heard a song. It was not

a casual song anyone might sing walking along the beach. It was a powerful, developed voice with a firm core of gravity, accustomed to vast halls and a large public. Neither the sand nor wind nor sea nor space could attenuate it. It was flung out with assurance, in defiance to them all, a vital hymn of equal strength to the elements.

The man who appeared had a body which was a full match to his voice, a perfect case for this instrument. He had a strong neck, a large head with high brow, wide shoulders and long legs. A full strong box for the vocal cords, good for resonance, thought Sabina, who had not moved, hoping he would walk by without seeing her and without interrupting this song from Tristan and Isolde.

As the song continued she found herself in the Black Forest of the German fairytales which she had read so avidly in her childhood. Giant trees, castles, horsemen, all out of proportion in a child's eyes.

The song ascended, swelled, gathered together all the turmoil of the sea, the rutilant gold carnival of the sun, rivalled the wind and flung its highest notes into space like the bridge span of a flamboyant rainbow. And then the incantation broke.

He had seen Sabina.

He hesitated.

Her silence as perfectly eloquent as his song, her immobility as flowing an essence of her meaning as his voice had been.

(Later he told her: if you had spoken then I would have walked away. You had the talent of letting everything else speak for you. It was because you were silent that I came up to you.)

She allowed him to continue his dream.

She watched him walk freely and easily up the sand dune, smiling. His eyes took their color from the sea. A moment ago she had seen the sea as a million diamond eyes and now only two, bluer, colder, approached her. If the sea and the sand and the sun had formed a man to incarnate the joyousness of the afternoon they would have spouted a man like this.

He stood before her blocking the sun, still smiling as she covered herself. The silence continued to transmit messages between them.

"Tristan and Isolde sounded more beautiful here than at the Opera," she said. And donned her bathing suit and her necklace quietly, as if this were the end of a performance of his voice and her body.

He sat down beside her. "There is only one place where it sounds better. The Black Forest itself, where the song was born."

By his accent she knew that he came from there, and that his physical resemblance to the Wagnerian hero was not accidental.

"I sang it there very often. There's an echo there, and I had the feeling the song was being preserved in hidden sources and that it will spring up again long after I am dead."

Sabina seemed to be listening to the echo of his song, and of his description of a place where there was memory, where the past itself was like a vast echo retaining experience; whereas here there was this great determination to dispose of memories and to live only in the present, as if memory were but a cumbersome baggage. That was what he meant, and Sabina understood.

Then her tidal movement caught her again, and she said impatiently: "Let's walk."

"I'm thirsty," he said. "Let's walk back to where I was sitting. I left a bag of oranges."

They descended the sand dunes sliding as if it were a hill of snow and they had been on skiis. They walked along the wet sand.

"I saw a beach once where each step you took made the phosphorous sparkle under the feet."

"Look at the sand-peckers," said the singer inaccurately, but Sabina liked his invention, and laughed.

"I came here to rest before my opening at the Opera."

They ate the oranges, swam, and walked again. Only at sundown did they lie on the sand.

She expected a violent gesture from him, in keeping with his large body, heavy arms, muscular neck.

He turned his eyes fully upon her, now a glacial blue; they were impersonal and seemed to gaze beyond her at all women who had dissolved into one, but who might, at any moment again become dissolved into all. This was the gaze Sabina had always encountered in Don Juan, everywhere, it was the gaze she mistrusted. It was the alchemy of desire fixing itself upon the incarnation of all women into Sabina for a moment but as easily by a second process able to alchemize Sabina into many others.

Her identity as the "unique" Sabina loved by Alan, was threatened. Her mistrust of his glance made the blood flow cold within her.

She examined his face to see if he divined that she was

nervous, that every moment of experience brought on this nervousness, almost paralyzing her.

But instead of a violent gesture he took hold of her finger tips with his smoothly designed hands, as if he were inviting her for an airy waltz, and said: "Your hands are cold."

He caressed the rest of her arm, kissing the nook between the elbows, the shoulders, and said: "Your body is feverishly hot. Have you had too much sun?"

To reassure him she said unguardedly: "Stage fright."

At this he laughed, mockingly, unbelieving, as she had feared he would. (There was only one man who believed she was afraid and at this moment she would have liked to run back to Alan, to run away from this mocking stranger whom she had attempted to deceive by her poise, her expert silences, her inviting eyes. This was too difficult to sustain and she would fail. She was straining, and she was frightened. She did not know how to regain prestige in his eyes, having admitted a weakness which the stranger mockingly disbelieved, and which was not in harmony with her provocative behaviour. This mocking laughter she was to hear once more when later he invited her to meet his closest friend, his companion in adventure, his brother Don Juan, as suave, as graceful and confident as himself. They had treated her merrily as one of their own kind, the adventuress, the huntress, the invulnerable woman, and it had offended her!)

When he saw she did not share his laughter, he became serious, lying at her side, but she was still offended and her heart continued to beat loudly with stage fright.

"I have to go back," she said, rising and shaking the

sand off with vehemence.

With immediate gallantry he rose, denoting a long habit of submission to women's whims. He rose and dressed himself, swung his leather bag over his shoulder and walked beside her, ironically courteous, impersonal, unaffected.

After a moment he said: "Would you like to meet me for dinner at the Dragon?"

"Not for dinner but later, yes. About ten or eleven."

He again bowed, ironically, and walked with cool eyes beside her. His nonchalance irritated her. He walked with such full assurance that he ultimately always obtained his desire, and she hated this assurance, she envied it.

When they reached the beach town everyone turned to gaze at them. The Bright Messenger, she thought, from the Black Forest of the fairytales. Breathing deeply, expanding his wide chest, walking very straight, and then this festive smile which made her feel gay and light. She was proud of walking at his side, as if bearing a trophy. As a woman she was proud in her feminine vanity, in her love of conquest. This vainglorious walk gave her an illusion of strength and power: she had charmed, won, such a man. She felt heightened in her own eyes, while knowing this sensation was not different than drunkenness, and that it would vanish like the ecstasies of drink, leaving her the next day even more shaky, even weaker at the core, deflated, defeated, possessing nothing within herself.

The core, where she felt a constant unsureness, this structure always near collapse which could so easily be

shattered by a harsh word, a slight, a criticism, which floundered before obstacles, was haunted by the image of catastrophe, by the same obsessional forebodings which she heard in Ravel's Waltz.

The waltz leading to catastrophe: swirling in spangled airy skirts, on polished floors, into an abyss, the minor notes simulating lightness, a mock dance, the minor notes always recalling that man's destiny was ruled by ultimate darkness.

This core of Sabina's was temporarily supported by an artificial beam, the support of vanity's satisfaction when this man so obviously handsome walked by her side, and everyone who saw him envied the woman who had charmed him.

When they separated he bowed over her hand in a European manner, with mock respect, but his voice was warm when he repeated: "You will come?" When none of his handsomeness, perfection and nonchalance had touched her, this slight hesitation did. Because he was for a moment uncertain, she felt him for a moment as a human being, a little closer to her when not altogether invulnerable.

She said: "Friends are waiting for me."

Then a slow to unfold but utterly dazzling smile illumined his face as he stood to his full height and saluted: "Change of guards at Buckingham Palace!"

By his tone of irony she knew he did not expect her to be meeting friends but most probably another man, another lover.

He would not believe that she wanted to return to her room to wash the sand out of her hair, to put oil over her sunburnt skin, to paint a fresh layer of polish on her nails, to relive every step of their encounter as she lay in the bath, in her habit of wanting to taste the intoxications of experience not once but twice.

To the girl she shared the room with she owed but a slight warning that she would be out that evening, but on this particular evening there was a third person staying with them for just one night, and this woman was a friend of Alan as well as hers; so her departure would be more complicated. Once more she would have to steal ecstasy and rob the night of its intoxications. She waited until they were both asleep and went silently out, but did not go towards the Main street where all her friends the artists would be walking and who might offer to join her. She leaped over the wharf's railing and slid down the wooden pole, scratching her hands and her dress against the barnacles, and leaped on to the beach. She walked along the wet sand towards the most brightly lighted of the wharves where the Dragon offered its neon lighted body to the thirsty night explorers.

None of her friends could afford to come there, where even the piano had discarded its modest covering and added the dance of its bare inner mechanism to the other motions, extending the pianist's realm from abstract notes to a disciplined ballet of reclining chess figures on agitated wires.

To reach the nightclub she had to climb large iron ladders planted on the glistening poles, on which her dress caught, and her hair. She arrived out of breath as if she had been diving from there and were returning after freeing herself from the clasp of the sea weeds. But no one noticed her except Philip, the spotlight being on the singer of cajoling blues.

A flush of pleasure showed even through the deep tan. He held a chair out for her and bent over to whisper: "I was afraid you were not coming. When I passed by your studio at ten o'clock, I didn't see any light, so I walked up and knocked at the window, not too hard, because I don't see well at night, and I was afraid I had made a mistake. There was no answer. I stumbled about in the dark . . . waited . . ."

At the terror that Philip might have awakened her friends, at the danger that had barely been averted, she felt fever mounting, the heat of the blood set off by danger. His handsomeness at night became a drug, and the image of his night blinded selfseeking her, touched her, and disarmed her. Her eyes now turned dark and rimmed with coal dust like those of oriental women. The eyelids had a bluish tint, and her eyebrows which she did not pluck, threw shadows which made her eyes' dark glints seem to come from a deeper source than during the day.

Her eyes absorbed the vivid modelling of his features, and the contrast between his strong head and the long fingered hands, hairless, covered by the finest down. He not only caressed her skin along her arm, but seemed to exert a subtle musician's pressure on the concealed nerves of an instrument he knew well, saying: "The beauty of your arm is exactly like that of your body. If I didn't know your body I would want it, just from seeing the shape of your arm."

Desire made a volcanic island, on which they lay in a

trance, feeling the subterranean whirls lying beneath them, dance floor and table and the magnetic blues uprooted by desire, the avalanches of the body's tremors. Beneath the delicate skin, the tendrils of secret hair, the identations and valleys of flesh, the volcanic lava flowed, desire incandescent, and where it burned the voices of the blues being sung became a harsh wilderness cry, bird and animal's untamed cry of pleasure and cry of danger and cry of fear and cry of childbirth and cry of wound pain from the same hoarse delta of nature's pits.

The trembling premonitions shaking the hand, the body, made dancing unbearable, waiting unbearable, smoking and talking unbearable, soon would come the untamable seizure of sensual cannibalism, the joyous epilepsies.

They fled from the eyes of the world, the singer's prophetic, harsh, ovarian prologues. Down the rusty bars of ladders to the undergrounds of the night propitious to the first man and woman at the beginning of the world, where there were no words by which to possess each other, no music for serenades, no presents to court with, no tournaments to impress and force a yielding, no secondary instruments, no adornments, necklaces, crowns to subdue, but only one ritual, a joyous, joyous, joyous, joyous impaling of woman on man's sensual mast.

She reopened her eyes to find herself lying at the bottom of a sail boat, lying over Philip's coat gallantly protecting her from sediments, water seepage and barnacles. Philip lies beside her, only his head is above hers, and his feet extend further down than hers. He lies asleep, content, breathing very deeply. She sits up in the moonlight, angry, restless, defeated. The fever had reached its peak, and waned separately from her desire, leaving it unfulfilled, stranded. High fever and no climax, — Anger, Anger — at this core which will not melt, while Sabina wills to be like man, free to possess and desire in adventure, to enjoy a stranger. Her body will not melt, will not obey her fantasy of freedom. It cheated her of the adventure she had pursued. The fever, the hope, the mirage, the suspended desire, unfulfilled, would remain with her all night and the next day, burn undimmed within her and make others who saw her say: "How sensual she is!"

Philip awakened and smiled gratefully. He had given and taken and was content.

Sabina lay thinking she would not see him again, and wishing desperately she might. He was talking about his childhood and his love of snow. He had loved to ski. Then without transition, some image came to disturb this idyllic scene and he said: "Women will never leave me alone."

Sabina said: "If you ever want to be with a woman who will not always expect you to make love, come to me. I will understand."

"You're wonderful to say that, Sabina. Women are so offended if you are not always ready and in the mood to play the romantic lover, when you look the part."

It was her words which brought him back the next day when he had confessed to her that he never spent more than one evening with a woman for "After that she begins to demand too much, to lay claims . . ."

He came and they walked to the sand dunes. He was talkative but always impersonal. Secretly Sabina hoped he might tell her something that would melt the unmeltable sensual core, that she might respond, that he might break through her resistance.

Then the absurdity of her expectation amazed her: seeking another kind of fusion because she had failed to achieve the sensual one, when what she wanted was only the sensual one, to reach man's freedom in adventure, to arrive at enjoyment without dependence which might liberate her from all her anxieties connected with love.

For a moment she saw her love anxieties as resembling those of a drug addict, of alcoholics, of gamblers. The same irresistible impulse, tension, compulsion and then depression following the yielding to the impulse, revulsion, bitterness, depression, and the compulsion once more . . .

Three times the sea, the sun, and the moon witnessed and mocked her efforts at truly possessing Philip, this adventure, this man whom other women so envied her.

And now in the city, in autumn purple, she was walking towards his apartment after a telephone call from him. The bells on the Indian ring he had given her were tinkling merrily.

She remembered her fear that he would vanish with the summer. He had not asked for her address. The day before he left, a friend arrived. He had spoken of this woman with reserve. Sabina had divined that she was the essential one. She was a singer, he had taught her, music bound them. Sabina heard in his voice a tone of respect which she did not like to inspire, but which was like Alan's tone when he talked about her. For this other woman Philip had the sympathy Alan had for Sabina. He spoke tenderly of her health not being good, to Sabina who had kept so fiercely the secret of being cold when they swam, or tired when they walked too long, or feverish in too much sun.

Sabina invented a superstitious game: if this woman were beautiful, then Sabina would not see him again. If not, if she was the steadfastly loved one, then Sabina could be the whim, the caprice, the drug, the fever.

When Sabina saw her she was amazed. The woman was not beautiful. She was pale, self-effacing. But in her presence Philip walked softly, happy, subdued in his happiness, less erect, less arrogant, but gently serene. No streaks of lightning in his ice-blue eyes, but a soft early morning glow.

And Sabina knew that when he would want fever he would call her.

Whenever she felt lost in the endless deserts of insomnia she would take up the labyrinthian thread of her life again from the beginning to see if she could find at what moment the paths had become confused.

Tonight she remembered the moon-baths, as if this had marked the beginning of her life instead of the parents, school, birthplace. As if they had determined the course of her life rather than inheritance or imitation of the parents. In the moon-baths perhaps, lay the secret motivation of her acts.

At sixteen Sabina took moon-baths, first of all because everyone else took sun-baths, and second, she admitted, because she had been told it was dangerous. The effect of moon-baths was unknown, but it was intimated that it might be the opposite of the sun's effect.

The first time she exposed herself she was frightened. What would the consequences be? There were many taboos against gazing at the moon, many old legends about the evil effects of falling asleep in moonlight. She knew that the insane found the full moon acutely disturbing, that some of them regressed to animal habits of howling at the moon. She knew that in astrology the moon ruled the night life of the unconscious, invisible to consciousness.

But then she had always preferred the night to the day.

Moonlight fell directly over her bed in the summer. She lay naked in it for hours before falling asleep, wondering what its rays would do to her skin, her hair, her eyes, and then deeper, to her feelings.

By this ritual it seemed to her that her skin acquired a different glow, a night glow, an artificial luminousness which showed its fullest effulgence only at night, in artificial light. People noticed it and asked her what was happening. Some suggested she was using drugs.

It accentuated her love of mystery. She meditated on this planet which kept a half of itself in darkness. She felt related to it because it was the planet of lovers. Her attraction for it, her desire to bathe in its rays, explained her repulsion for home, husband and children. She began to imagine she knew the life which took place on the moon. Homeless, childless, free lovers, not even tied to each other.

The moon-baths crystallized many of Sabina's desires and orientations. Up to that moment she had only experienced a simple rebellion against the lives which surrounded her, but now she began to see the forms and colors of other lives, realms much deeper and stranger and remote to be discovered, and that her denial of ordinary life had a purpose: to send her off like a rocket into other forms of existence. Rebellion was merely the electric friction accumulating a charge of power that would launch her into space.

She understood why it angered her when people spoke of life as One life. She became certain of myriad lives within herself. Her sense of time altered. She felt acutely and with grief, the shortness of life's physical span. Death was terrifyingly near, and the journey towards it, vertiginous; but only when she considered the lives around her, accepting their time tables, clocks, measurements. Everything they did constricted time. They spoke of one birth, one childhood, one adolescence, one romance, one marriage, one maturity, one aging, one death, and then transmitted the monotonous cycle to their children. But Sabina, activated by the moonrays, felt germinating in her the power to extend time in the ramifications of a myriad lives and loves, to expand the journey to infinity, taking immense and luxurious detours as the courtesan depositor of multiple desires. The seeds of many lives, places, of many women in herself were fecundated by the moon-rays because they came from that limitless night life which we usually perceive only in our dreams, containing roots reaching for all the magnificences of the past, transmitting the rich sediments into the present, projecting them into the future.

In watching the moon she acquired the certainty of the expansion of time by depth of emotion, range and infinite multiplicity of experience.

It was this flame which began to burn in her, in her eyes and skin, like a secret fever, and her mother looked at her in anger and said: "You look like a consumptive." The flame of accelerated living by fever glowed in her and drew people to her as the lights of night life drew passersby out of the darkness of empty streets.

When she did finally fall asleep it was the restless sleep of the night watchman continuously aware of danger and of the treacheries of time seeking to cheat her by permitting clocks to strike the passing hours when she was not awake to grasp their contents.

She watched Alan closing the windows, watched him light the lamps, and fasten the lock on the door which let to the porch. All the sweet enclosures, and yet Sabina, instead of slipping languorously into the warmth and gentleness, felt a sudden restlessness like that of a ship pulling against its moorings.

The image of the ship's cracking, restless bones arrived on the waves of Debussy's Ile Joyeuse which wove around her all the mists and dissolutions of remote islands. The model notes arrived charged like a caravan of spices, gold mitres, ciboriums and chalices bearing messages of delight setting the honey flowing between the thighs, erecting sensual minarets on men's bodies as they lay flat on the sand. Debris of stained glass wafted up by the seas, splintered by the radium shafts of the sun and the waves and tides of sensuality covered their bodies, desires folding in every lapping wave like an accordion of aurora borealis in the blood. She saw an unreachable dance, at which men and women were dressed in rutilant colors, she saw their gayety, their relations to each other as unparalleled in splendor.

By wishing to be there where it was more marvellous she made the near, the palpable seem like an obstruction, a delay to the more luminous life awaiting her, the incandescent personages kept waiting.

The present — Alan, with his wrists hidden in silky brown hair, his long neck always bending towards her like a very tree of faithfulness — was murdered by the insistent, whispering interfering dream, a compass pointing to mirages flowing in the music of Debussy like an endless beckoning, alluring, its voices growing fainter if she did not listen with her whole being, its steps lighter if she did not follow, its promises, its sighs of pleasure growing clearer as they penetrated deeper regions of her body directly through the senses bearing on airy canopies all the fluttering banners of gondolas and divertissements.

Debussy's Clair de Lune shone on other cities . . . She wanted to be in Paris, the city propitious to lovers, where policemen smiled absolution and taxi drivers never interrupted a kiss . . .

Debussy's Clair de Lune shone upon many stranger's faces, upon many Iles Joyeuses, music festivals in the black forest, marimbas praying at the feet of smoking volcanoes, frenzied intoxicating dances in Haiti, and she was not there. She was lying in a room with closed windows under a lamplight.

The music grew weary of calling her, the black notes bowed to her inertia ironically in the form of a pavane for a defunct infanta, and dissolved. All she could hear now were the fog horns on the Hudson from ships she would never be able to board.

Sabina emerged a week later dressed in purple, and waited for one of the Fifth Avenue buses which allowed smoking. Once seated she opened an overfull handbag and brought out a Hindu ring with minuscule bells on it, and slipped it on in place of her wedding ring. The wedding ring was pushed to the bottom of the bag. Each gesture she made was now accompanied by the tinkling of bells.

At Sixty-Fourth Street she leaped out of the bus before it had entirely stopped and her walk had changed. She now walked swiftly, directly, with a power and vigor to her hips. She walked with her whole foot flat on the ground as the latins and the negroes do. Whereas on her way to Alan's her shoulders had been bowed, now they were vigorously thrown back and she was breathing deeply, feeling her breasts pushing against the purple dress.

The ripples of her walk started from the pelvis and hips, a strong undulation like waves of muscles flowing from the feet to the knees, to the hips and back to the waist. She walked with her entire body as if to gain momentum for an event in which her entire body would participate. On her face there was no longer any bewilderment, but a vehemence which caused people to stop and glance at her face as if they had been touched by a magnet.

The evening lights were being turned on, and at this hour Sabina felt like the city, as if all the lights were turned on at once causing a vast illumination. There were lights on her hair, in her eyes, on her nails, on the ripples of her purple dress now turning black.

When she finally reached the apartment, she realized

she still did not know whether he lived alone.

He guided her into a room which looked like him and had been arranged for him alone. His skiing trophies hung on the walls: on a Viennese curtain of damask hung a whole army of tin soldiers in army formation. On the piano lay stacks of music in disorder, and in the center of the room, under an umbrella hung open from the ceiling, a partly constructed telescope.

"I want to see the stars with my own handmade telescope. I'm now polishing the glass. It takes a long, long time and a great deal of patience."

"But the umbrella!" exclaimed Sabina laughing.

"The children in the apartment above mine jump around and fine particles of plaster kept falling over my glass, scratching it. The finest grain of dust can spoil a whole day's polishing."

She understood his desire to observe the planets through an instrument made by his own hands. She was eager to see it finished and wanted to know how long it would take. Absorbed by the telescope they behaved like friends, and for a moment abandoned the tense challenges and teasings of conquest.

In this mood they undressed. Philip was playfully inventing endless grimaces, as children do. He loved to make himself grotesque as if he were tired of being always flawlessly handsome. He could turn himself into Frankenstein.

Sabina laughed, but uneasily, fearful that if his handsomeness truly vanished she would no longer desire him, aware of the evanescence and fragility of this desire. If the singer of Tristan and Isolde singing in the Black

Forest of the fairytales disappeared, what would she desire then?

Then his cool eyes became aware of the intensity of her eyes and they stirred him. His detachment was ignited by the smouldering violence in her. He did not want fires or explosions of feeling in a woman, but he wanted to know it was there. He wanted the danger of touching it off only in the dark depths of her flesh, but without rousing a heart that would bind him. He often had fantasies of taking a woman whose arms were bound behind her back.

Once he had seen a heavy storm cloud settle over a twin-nippled mountain, so closely knit, like an embrace and he had said: "Wonderful copulation, the mountain has no arms!"

Now he grew tired of making faces, and having resumed the perfectly modelled features, he bent over her to pay homage to her body.

And then it happened like a miracle, this pulsation of pleasure unequalled by the most exalted musicians, the summits of perfection in art or science or wars, unequalled by the most regal beauties of nature, this pleasure which transformed the body into a high tower of fireworks gradually exploding into fountains of delight through the senses.

She opened her eyes to contemplate the piercing joy of her liberation: she was free, free as man was, to enjoy without love.

Without any warmth of the heart, as a man could, she had enjoyed a stranger.

And then she remembered what she had heard men

say: "Then I wanted to leave."

She gazed at the stranger lying naked beside her and saw him as a statue she did not want to touch again. As a statue he lay far from her, strange to her, and there welled in her something resembling anger, regret, almost a desire to take this gift of herself back, to efface all traces of it to banish it from her body. She wanted to become swiftly and cleanly detached from him, to disentangle and unmingle what had been fused for a moment, their breaths, skins,exhalations,and body's essences.

She slid very softly out of the bed, dressed with adroit soundlessness while he slept. She tiptoed to the bathroom.

On the shelf she found face powder, comb, lipstick in shell rose wrappings. She smiled at them. Wife? Mistress? How good it was to contemplate these objects without the lightest tremor of regret, envy or jealousy. That was the meaning of freedom. Free of attachment, dependency and the capacity for pain. She breathed deeply and felt she had found this source of pleasure for good. Why had it been so difficult? So difficult that she had often simulated this pleasure?

While combing her hair, and repainting her eyelashes, she enjoyed this bathroom, this neutral zone of safety. While moving between men, lovers, she always entered with pleasure a natural safety zone (in the bus, in the taxi, on the way from one to another, at this moment the bathroom) safe from grief. If she had loved Philip, how each one of these objects, face powder, hair pins, comb, each one would have hurt her!

(He is not to be trusted. I am only passing by. I am on my way to another place, another life, where he cannot even find me, claim me. How good not to love; I remember the eyes of the woman who met Philip at the beach. Her eyes were in a panic as she looked at me. She wondered if I were the one who would take him away. And how this panic disappeared at the tone of Philip's voice as he introduced her: "Meet Dona Juana." The woman had understood the tone of his voice and the fear had vanished from her eyes.)

What new reassurance Sabina felt as she laced her sandals, swirled her cape and smoothed her long, straight hair. She was not only free from danger but free for a quick get-away. That is what she called it. (Philip had observed he had never seen a woman dress so quickly, never seen a woman gather up her belongings as quickly and never forgetting a single one!)

How she had learned to flush love letters down the toilet, to leave no hairs on the borrowed comb, to gather up hair pins, to erase traces of lipstick anywhere, to brush off clouds of face powder.

Her eyes like the eyes of a spy.

Her habits like the habits of a spy. How she lay all her clothes on one chair, as if she might be called away suddenly and must not leave any traces of her presence.

She knew all the trickeries in this war of love.

And her neutral zone, the moment when she belonged to none, when she gathered her dispersed self together again. The moment of non-loving, non-desiring. The moment when she took flight, if the man had admired another woman passing by, or talked too long about an old love, the little offences, the small stabs, a mood of indifference, a small unfaithfulness, a small treachery, all of them were warnings of possibly larger ones, to be counter-acted by an equal or larger or total unfaithfulness, her own, the most magnificent of counterpoisons, prepared in advance for the ultimate emergencies. She was accumulating a supply of treacheries, so that when the shock came, she would be prepared: "I was not taken unaware, the trap was not sprung on my naivete, on my foolish trustingness. I had already betrayed. To be always ahead, a little ahead of the expected betrayals by life. To be there first and therefore prepared . . ."

When she returned to the room Philip was still asleep. It was the end of the afternoon and the rain sent cooler winds over the bed, but she felt no desire to cover or shelter him, or to give him warmth.

She had only been away five days but because of all the emotions and experiences which had taken place, all the inner expansions and explorations, Sabina felt that she had been away for many years. Alan's image had receded far into the past, and a great fear of complete loss of him assailed her. Five days containing so many changes within her body and feelings lengthened the period of absence, added unmeasurable mileage to her separation from Alan.

Certain roads one took emotionally also appeared on the map of the heart as travelling away from the center, and ultimately leading to exile.

Driven by this mood, she appeared at his home.

"Sabina! I'm so happy. I didn't expect you for another week. What happened? Nothing went wrong?"

He was there. Five days had not altered his voice, the all-enveloping expression of his eyes. The apartment had not changed. The same book was still open by his bed, the same magazines had not yet been thrown away. He had not finished some fruit she had bought the last time she had been there. Her hands caressed the overfull ash trays, her fingers designed rivers of meditation on the coats of dust on the table. Here living was gradual, organic, without vertiginous descents or ascents.

As she stood there the rest of her life appeared like a fantasy. She sought Alan's hand and searched for the familiar freckle on his wrist. She felt a great need to take a bath before he touched her, to wash herself rigorously of other places, other hands, other odors.

Alan had obtained for her, as a surprise, some records of drumming and singing from the Ile Joyeuse. They listened to the drumming which began at first remotely as if playing in a distant village smothered in jungle vines. At first like small children's steps running through dry rushes, and then heavier steps on hollow wood, and then sharp powerful fingers on the drum skins, and suddenly a mass of crackling stumpings, animal skins slapped and knuckled, stirred and pecked so swiftly there was no time for echoes. Sabina saw the ebony and cinnamon bodies through which the structure of the bones never showed, glistening with the sea's wild baths, leaping and dancing as quick as the necklaces of drum beats, in emerald greens, indigo blue, tangerines in all the colors of fruits and flowers, flaming eucalyptus of flesh.

There were places where only the beat of the blood guided the body, where there was no separation from the speed of wind, the tumult of waves, and the sun's orgies. The voices rich with sap sang joyously . . . cascabel . . . guyabana . . .chinchinegrites . . .

"I wish we could go there together," said Sabina.

Alan looked at her reproachfully as if it hurt him to be obliged to remind her: "I can't leave my work. Later this year perhaps . . ."

Sabina's eyes grew fixed. Alan interpreted it as disappointment and added: "Please be patient, Sabina."

But Sabina's gaze was not transfixed by disappointment. It was the fixation of the visionary. She was watching a mirage take form, birds were being born with new names: "cuchuchito", "Pito real". They perched on trees called "liquidambar", and over her head stretched a roof made of palm leaves tied with reeds. *Later was always too late; late did not exist.* There was only great distance to overcome to reach the inaccessible. The drums had come bearing the smell of cinnamon skins in a dance of heartbeats. They would soon bring an invitation which she would not refuse.

When Alan looked at her face again, her eyelashes had dropped in a simulacrum of obedience. He felt the imminence of departure had been averted by a sudden docility. He did not observe that her quiescence was already in itself, a form of absence. She was already inhabiting the Ile Joyeuse.

Perhaps because of this, when she heard drumming as she walked along McDougall Street she found it natural to stop, to climb down the steps into a cellar room of orange walls and sit on one of the fur covered drums.

The drummers were playing in complete self absorption intended for a ritual, seeking their own trances. A smell of spices came from the kitchen and gold ear rings

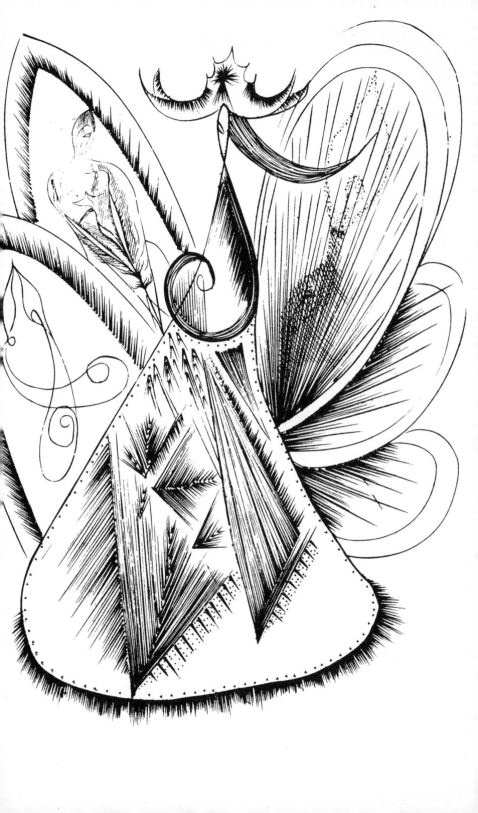

danced over the steaming dishes.

The voices started an incantation to Alalle, became the call of birds, the call of animals, rapids falling over rocks, reeds dipping their fingered roots into the lagoon waters. The drums beat so fast the room turned into a forest of tap-dancing foliage, wind chimes cajoling Alalle, the dispenser of pleasure.

Among the dark faces there was one pale one. A grandmother from France or Spain, and a stream of shell-white had been added to the cauldron of ebony, leaving his hair as black but with a reflector depth like that of a black mirror. His head was round, his brow wide, his cheeks full, his eyes soft and brilliant. His fingers on the drum nimble yet fluid, playing with a vehemence which rippled from his hips and shoulders.

Sabina could see him swimming, squatting over a fire by the beach, leaping, climbing trees. No bones showing, only the smoothness of the South Sea islander, muscles strong but invisible as in cats.

The diffusion of color on his face also gave his gestures a nerveless firmness, quite different from the nervous staccato of the other drummers. He came from the island of softness, of soft wind and warm sea, where violence lay in abeyance and exploded only in cycles. The life too sweet, too lulling, too drugging for continuous anger.

When they stopped playing they sat at a table near hers, and talked in an elaborate, formal, sixteenth century colonial Spanish, in the stilted language of old ballads. They practised an elaborate politeness which made Sabina smile. The stylization imposed by the conquerors upon African depths, was like a baroque ornamentation on a thatched palm leaf hut. One of them, the darkest one, wore a stiff white collar, and had a long stemmed umbrella by his chair. He held his hat with great care on his knees, and in order not to disturb the well ironed lines of his suit he drummed almost entirely from the wrists and moved his head from left to right of the starched collar, separate from his shoulders like that of a Balinese dancer.

She was tempted to disrupt their politeness, to break the polished surface of their placidity with her extravagance. As she shook her cigarette on her vanity case, the Hindu ring given to her by Philip, tinkled, and the pale-faced drummer turned his face towards her and smiled, as if this fragile sound were an inadequate response to his drumming.

When he returned to his singing an invisible web had already been spun between their eyes. She no longer watched his hands on the drumskin but his mouth. His lips were full, evenly so, rich but firmly designed, but the way he held them was like an offer of fruit. They never closed tightly or withdrew by the slightest contraction, but remained offered.

His singing was offered to her in this cup of his mouth, and she drank it intently, without spilling a drop of this incantation of desire. Each note was the brush of his mouth upon her. His singing grew exalted and the drumming deeper and sharper and it showered upon her heart and body. Drum - drum - drum- drum - drum - upon her heart, she was the drum, her skin was taut under his hands, and the drumming vibrated through the rest of her body. Wherever he rested his eyes, she felt the drumming of his fingers upon her stomach, her breasts, her hips. His eyes rested on her naked feet in sandals and they beat an answering rhythm. His eyes rested on the indented waist where the hips began to swell out, and she felt possessed by his song. When he stopped drumming he left his hands spread on the drumskin, as if he did not want to remove his hands from her body, and they continued to look at each other and then away as if fearing everyone had seen the desire flowing between them.

But when they danced he changed. The direct, the inescapable way he placed his knees between hers, as if implanting the rigidity of his desire. He held her firmly, so encompassed that every movement they made was made as one body. He held her head against his, with a physical finiteness, as if for eternity. His desire became a center of gravity, a final welding. He was not much taller than she but held himself proudly and when she raised her eyes into his, his eyes thrust into her very being, so sensually direct that she could not bear their radiance, their claim. Fever shone in his face like moonlight. At the same time a strange wave of anger appeared which she felt and could not understand.

When the dance ended, his bow was a farewell, as finite as his desire had been.

She waited, in anguish and bewilderment.

He went back to his singing and drumming but no longer offered them to her.

Yet she knew he had desired her, and why was he destroying it now? Why?

Her anxiety grew so violent she wanted to stop the

drumming, stop the others from dancing. But she checked this impulse, sensing it would estrange him. There was his pride. There was this strange mixture of passivity and aggressivity in him. In music he had been glowing and soft and offered; in the dance, tyrannical. She must wait. She must respect the ritual.

The music stopped, he came to her table, sat down and gave her a smile mixed with a contraction of pain.

"I know," he said. "I know . . ."

"You know?"

"I know, but it cannot be," he said very gently. And then suddenly the anger overflowed: "For me, it's everything or nothing. I've known this before . . . a-woman like you. Desire. It's desire, but not for *me*. *You don't know me*. It's for my race, it's for a sensual power we have."

He reached for her wrists and spoke close to her face: "It destroys me. Everywhere desire, and in the ultimate giving, withdrawal. Because I am African. What do you know of me? I sing and drum and you desire me. But I'm not an entertainer. I'm a mathematician, a composer, a writer." He looked at her severely, the fullness of his mouth difficult to compress in anger but his eyes lashing: "You wouldn't come to Ile Joyeuse and be my wife and bear me black children and wait patiently upon my negro grandmother!"

Sabina answered him with equal vehemence, throwing her hair away from her face, and lowering the pitch of her voice until it sounded like an insult: "I'll tell you one thing: if it were only what you say, I've had that, and it didn't hold me, it was not enough, it was magnificent, but it didn't hold me. You're destroying everything, with your bitterness, you're angry, you've been hurt . . ."

"Yes, it's true, I've been hurt, and by a woman who resembled you. When you first came in, I thought it was she . . ."

"My name is Sabina."

"I don't trust you, I don't trust you at all."

But when she rose to dance with him, he opened his arms and as she rested her head on his shoulder he looked down at her face drained of all anger and bitterness.

Mambo's studio was situated in Patchen Place, a street without issue. An iron railing half blocked its entrance, like an entrance to a prison. The houses all being identical added to this impression of an institution where all variations in the human personality would be treated like eccentricities and symptoms of disintegration.

Sabina hated this street. She always considered it a trap. She was certain that the lie detector had seen her enter and would wait at the gate to see her come out. How simple it would be for him to find out who lived there, whom she visited, which house she came out of in the morning.

She imagined him searching every house, reading all the names on the letter boxes: E. E. Cummings, Djuna Barnes, Mambo of Mambo's Nightclub, known to everyone.

At dawn, the lie detector himself would see her come out of the house, holding her cape tightly around her against the morning sharpness, her hair not smoothly combed, and her eyes not fully opened.

Any other street but this one.

Once in the early summer, she had been awakened by a painful tension of the nerves. All the windows were open. It was near dawn. The little street was absolutely silent. She could hear the leaves shivering on the trees. Then a cat wailing. Why had she awakened? Was there any danger? Was Alan watching at the gate?

She heard a woman's voice call out distinctly: "Betty! Betty!" And a voice answered in the muffled tones of half sleep: "What's the matter?"

"Betty! There's a man hiding in one of the doorways.

I saw him sneak in."

"Well . . . what do you want me to do about it? He's just a drunk getting home."

"No Betty. He was trying to hide when I leaned out of the window. Ask Tom to go and see. I'm frightened."

"Oh, don't be childish. Go to sleep. Tom worked late last night. I can't wake him. The man can't get in anyhow, unless you press the button and let him in!"

"But he'll be there when I go to work. He'll wait there. Call Tom."

"Go to sleep."

Sabina began to tremble. She was certain it was Alan. Alan was waiting down below, to see her come out. For her this was the end of the world. Alan was the core of her life. These other moments of fever were moments in a dream: unsubstantial and vanishing as quickly as they came. But if Alan repudiated her, it was the death of Sabina. Her existence in Alan's eyes was her only true existence. To say to herself: Alan cast me off, was like saying: Alan killed me.

The caresses of the night before were acutely marvellous, like all the multicolored flames from an artful fireworks, bursts of exploded suns and neons within the body, flying comets aimed at all the centers of delight, shooting stars of piercing joys, and yet if she said: "I will stay here and live with Mambo forever," it was like the children she had seen trying to stand under the showers of sparks from the fireworks lasting one instant and covering them with ashes.

She saw two scenes before her eyes: Alan sobbing as he had sobbed at the death of his father, and this image caused her an intolerable pain. And the second image was Alan angry, as he had never shown himself to her but to others, and this was equally intolerable; both equally annihilating.

It was not dawn yet. What could she do? Her anxiety was so great she could not continue to lie there in silence. How would she explain to Mambo her leaving so early in the morning? Nevertheless she rose quietly after sliding gradually out of bed, and dressed. She was trembling and her clothes slipped awkwardly between her fingers.

She must go and see who was the man hiding in the doorway. She could not bear the suspense.

She left the apartment slowly, noiselessly. She walked barefoot down the stairs, carrying her sandals. When one step creaked, she stopped. Perspiration showed on her eyebrows. A feeling of utter weakness kept her hands trembling. She finally reached the door and saw a man's outline behind the frosted glass of the door. He stood there smoking a pipe as Alan smoked it. Sabina's heart was paralyzed. She knew why she had always hated this street without issue. She stood there fully ten minutes, paralyzed by terror and guilt, by regrets for what she was losing.

"It's the end of the world," she whispered.

As if she were about to die, she summarized her existence: the heightened moments of passion dissolved as unimportant in the face of the loss of Alan as if this love were the core of her existence.

Formulating this, the anguish increased to the point where she could no longer stand still. She pushed the door open violently.

A stranger stood there, with red, blood-shot eyes and unsteady legs. He was frightened by her sudden appearance and muttered, leaning backwards: "Can't find my name on the doorbell, lady, can you help me?"

Sabina looked at him with a wild fury and ran past him, the corner of her cape slapping his face.

Mambo reproached her constantly: "You don't love me". He felt that she embraced in him, kissed on his lips the music, the legends the trees, the drums of the island he came from, that she sought to possess ardently both his body and his island, that she offered her body to his hands as much as to tropical winds, and that the undulations of pleasure resembled those of swimmers in tropical seas. She savoured on his lips his island spices and it was from his island, too, that he had learned his particular way of caressing her, a silken voluptuousness without harshness or violence, like the form of his island body on which no bone showed.

Sabina did not feel guilty for drinking of the tropics through Mambo's body: she felt a more subtle shame, that of bringing him a fabricated Sabina, feigning a single love.

Tonight when the drug of caresses whirled them into space, free — free for an instant of all the interferences to complete union created by human beings themselves, she would give him an undisguised Sabina.

When their still throbbing bodies lay side by side, there was always silence, and in this silence each one began to weave the separating threads, to disunite what had been united, to return to each what had been for a moment equally shared.

There were essences of caresses which could penetrate the heaviest insulations, filtering through the heaviest defences, but these, so soon after the exchange of desires, could be destroyed like the seeds of birth.

Mambo proceeded to this careful labor by renewing his secret accusation against Sabina, that she sought only pleasure, that she loved in him only the island man, the swimmer and the drummer, that she never touched in him, or ardently desired, or took into her body, the artist that he most valued in himself, the composer of music which was a distillation of the barbaric themes of his origin.

He was a run-away from his own island, seeking awareness, seeking shading and delicate balances as in the music of Debussy, and at his side lay Sabina, feverishly dispersing all the delicacies as she demanded: "Drum! Mambo, drum! Drum for me."

Sabina, too, was slipping out of the burning moment which had almost welded their differences. Her secret self unveiled and naked in his arms must be costumed once more for what she felt in the silence was his withdrawal and silent accusations.

Before he could speak and harm her with words while she lay naked and exposed, while he prepared a judgment, she was preparing her metamorphosis, so that whatever Sabina he struck down she could abandon like a disguise, shedding the self he had seized upon and say: "That was not me."

Any devastating words addressed to the Sabina he had possessed, the primitive one, could not reach her then; she was already halfway out of the forest of their desire, the core already far away, invulnerable, protected by flight. What remained was a costume: it was piled on the floor of his room, and empty of her.

Once in an ancient city in South America, Sabina had seen streets which had been ravaged by an earthquake. Nothing was left but facades, as in Chirico paintings, the facades of granite had remained with doors and windows half unhinged, opening unexpectedly not upon a household nestled around a hearth but whole families camping under the sky, protected from strangers only by one wall and door, but otherwise completely free of walls or roofs from the other three sides.

She realized that it was this illimitable space she had expected to find in every lover's room, the sea, the mountains visible all around, the world shut off on one side. A hearth without roof or walls, growing between trees, a floor through which wild flowers pushed to show smiling faces, a column housing stray birds, temples and pyramids and baroque churches in the distance.

But when she saw four walls and a bed pushed against the corner as if it had been flying and had collided against an obstacle, she did not feel as other voyagers: "I have arrived at my destination and can now remove my travelling costume" but: "I have been captured and from here, sooner or later, I must escape."

No place, no human being could bear to be gazed at with the critical eye of the absolute, as if they were obstacles to the reaching of a place or person of greater value created by the imagination. This was the blight she inflicted upon each room when she asked herself: "Am I to live here forever? This was the blight, the application of the irrevocable, the endless fixation upon a place or relationship. It aged it prematurely, it accelerated the process of decay by staleness. A chemical death ray, this concentrate of time, inflicting the fear of stasis like a consuming ray, deteriorating at the high speed of a hundred years per minute.

At this moment she was aware of her evil, of an invisible crime equal to murder in life. It was her secret sickness, one she believed incurable, unnamable.

Having touched the source of death, she turned back to her source of life; it was only in Stravinsky's "Firebird" that Sabina found her unerring musical autobiography. It was only here she could find the lost Sabina, her self-revelation.

Even when the first sensual footsteps of the orange bird first appeared, phosphorescent tracks along magnolia forests, she recognized her first sensations, the adolescent stalking of emotion, of its shadow first of all, the echo of its dazzling presence, not yet daring to enter the circle of frenzy.

She recognized the first prologue waltzes, the paintings on glass which might shatter at the touch of warm hands, the moon's haloes around featureless heads, the preparations for festivities and the wild drums announcing feasts of the hearts and senses. She recognized the crimson suspenses, the elevations which heightened the pulse, the wind which thrust its hieroglyphs through the swan necks of the trombones.

The fireworks were mounted on wire bodies waving amorous arms, tip-toeing on the purple tongues of the Holy Ghost, leaping out of captivity, Mercury's wings of orange on pointed torches hurled like javelins into space sparring through the clouds, the purple vulvas of the night.

On many of the evenings Sabina spent with Mambo they did not go anywhere.

On evenings when Sabina had agreed to return to Alan at midnight, her going out with a friend would not have been fatal or too difficult to explain; but there were evenings (when she wanted to spend a few whole nights with her lover) when she had been obliged to say she was travelling, and then when Mambo suggested: "Let's go to a movie," the conflict was started. She did not like to answer: "I don't want Alan to see me." This made her feel like a child being watched, or a woman in a state of subjection, so much did her feelings about Alan seem not like those of a woman wanting to be faithful or loyal but those of an adolescent escaping home for some forbidden games. She could only see Alan as a kind father who might become angry at her lies and punish her. She would also, if she mentioned Alan's rights, be forced to confess to Mambo the division in her affections. At times her lies seemed to her like the most intricate act of protectiveness instead of the greatest treachery. Other days she felt tempted to confess, but would be blocked by the knowledge that even if she were forgiven, Alan would expect then a change of life and this she knew she was powerless to achieve.

At mention of the movies she would assent, but as if it were a game of chance she were playing, each time that Mambo suggested one movie, or another, or still another, she weighed them not so much for their qualities as movies, but according to what quarter of the city they were shown at, whether or not it was a movie Alan might care to see, whether it was near at hand (knowing Alan was lazy about going uptown). If she were with Alan she would have to try and remember the movies Mambo had seen, or the ones he wanted to see, and knowing how fanatical he was about movies, to gauge even those he might see twice.

Ultimately, like a gambler, she had to question her instinct.

Once seated at the movies her anxiety increased. Alan might have liked this movie enough to want to see it again, or a friend might have persuaded him to make the effort to go uptown. Could Mambo be sitting in the audience while she sat with Alan, could he have seen her walking down the aisle?

Sometimes she discarded her anxiety as nervousness. At other times she was compelled to go to the ladies' room at the very beginning in order to be able to walk slowly and carefully down the aisle examining the crowd from behind before settling down beside Mambo or Alan. This would relieve her anxiety for awhile, until some fragment of the movie story itself would reawaken it, if a lie were pictured, a false situation, exposure. Above all if it were a spy story.

It was when she saw the lives of spies that she realized fully the tension with which she lived every moment, equal to theirs. The fear of committing themselves, of sleeping too soundly, of talking in their sleep, of carelessness of accent or behaviour, the need for continuous pretending, quick improvisations of motivations, quick justifications of their presence here or there.

It seemed to Sabina that she could have offered her services or been of great value in that profession.

*I am an international spy in the house of love.*

When the anxiety became absolutely intolerable it was transmuted into playfulness. The excitement and risks appeared as a highly flavored, highly humorous game. Then she shifted her position entirely to that of a child escaping surveillance and being amused by her own ingenuity. Then she passed from secrecy to a need of boasting openly of her manoeuvres and would describe them with such gayety that it would shock her hearers. Both anxiety and humor became interchangeable. The pretenses, escapades, trickeries seemed to her in her humorous moods like gay and gallant efforts at protecting everyone from the cruelties of existence for which she was not responsible. Wits and good acting were employed for such justifiable ends: to protect human beings from unbearable truths.

But no one who listened ever shared her sudden gayety: in their glances she read condemnations. Her laughter seemed a desecration, a mockery of what should be considered tragic. She could see in their eyes the wish that she should fall from this incandescent trapeze on which she walked with the aid of delicate Japanese paper umbrellas, for no guilty party has a right to such adroitness and to live only by its power to balance over the rigidities of life which dictated a choice, according to its taboos against multiple lives. No one would share with her this irony and playfulness against the rigidities of life itself; no one would applaud when she succeeded by her ingenuity in defeating life's limitations.

These moments when she reached a humorous peak above the morass of dangers, the smothering swamps of guilt, were the ones when everyone left her alone, unabsolved; they seemed to be awaiting her hour of punishment after living like a spy in the house of many loves, for avoiding exposure, for defeating the sentinels watching definite boundaries, for passing without passports and permits from one love to another.

Every spy's life had ended in ignominious death.

She stood waiting for the light to change at the cross-road of the beach town.

What startled Sabina and made her examine the cyclist waiting beside her was the extraordinary brilliance of his large eyes. They shone with a wet, silver sparkle which was almost frightening, because it highlighted the tumultuous panic close to the surface. The molten silver was disquieting, like blinding reflectors on the edge of annihilation by darkness. She was caught in the contagion of this panic, the transparent film of precious stone trembling, about to be sucked in by a hidden cyclone.

It was only later that she noticed the delicately chiseled face, the small nose, the mouth modelled by gentleness, unrelated to the deeper disturbance of the eyes, a very young man's mouth, a pure design on the face not yet enslaved by his feelings. These feelings not yet known to him, had not yet acid-bitten through his body. His gestures were free and nimble, the gestures of an adolescent, restless and light. The eyes alone contained all the fever.

He had driven his bicycle like a racing car or an airplane. He had come down upon her as if he did not see trees, cars, people, and almost overlooked the stop signal.

To free herself of the shock his eyes had given her she sought to diminish their power by thinking: "They are just beautiful eyes, they are just passionate eyes, young men rarely have such passionate eyes, they're just more alive than other eyes." But no sooner had she said this to herself to exorcise his spell than a deeper instinct in her added: "He has seen something other young men have not seen."

The red light changed to green; he gave a wild spurt to his pedalling, so swift that she had no time to step on the curb then just as wildly stopped and asked her the way to the beach in a breathless voice which seemed to miss a beat. The voice matched the eyes as his tan, healthy smooth skin did not.

The tone in which he asked directions was as if the beach were a shelter to which he was speeding away from grave dangers.

He was no handsomer than the other young men she had seen in the place, but his eyes left a memory and stirred in her a wild rebellion against the place. With bitter irony she remembered ruins she had seen in Guatemala, and an American visitor saying: "I hate ruins, I hate dilapidation, tombs." But this new town at the beach was infinitely more static and more disintegrated than the ancient ruins. The clouds of monotony, uniformity which hung over the new, neat mansions, the impeccable lawns, the dustless garden furniture. The men and women at the beach, all in one dimension, without any magnetism to bring them together, zombies of civilization, in elegant dress with dead eyes.

Why was she here? Waiting for Alan to end his work, Alan who had promised to come. But the longing for other places kept her awake.

She walked and collided against a sign which read: "This is the site of the most costly Church on Long Island."

She walked. At midnight the town was deserted. Everyone was at home with bottles from which they hoped to extract a gayety bottled elsewhere.

"It's the kind of drinking one does at Wakes," thought Sabina, looking into the bars, where limp figures clutched at bottles containing oblivion.

At one o'clock she looked for a drug store to buy sleeping pills. They were closed. She walked. At two o'clock she was worn out but still tormented by a place which refused to have feasts on the street, dances, fire works, orgies of guitars, marimbas, shouts of delight, tournaments of poetry and courtships.

At three o'clock she swung towards the beach to ask the moon why she had allowed one of her night children to become so lost in a place long ago deprived of human life.

A car stopped beside her, and a very tall, white-haired Irish policeman addressed her courteously.

"Can I give you a lift home?"

"I couldn't sleep," said Sabina. "I was looking for a drug store to buy sleeping pills, or aspirin. They're all closed. I was trying to walk until I felt sleepy . . ."

"Boy trouble?" he said, his white-haired head very gallantly held with a suave rectitude which did not come from his policeman's training but from some deeper pride in rectitude itself as the image of man's erotic pride.

But the words so inadequate that they inhibited whatever she would have liked to confide in him, for fear of another adolescent stunted comment. His appearance of maturity was belied by the clumsy words. So she said vaguely: "I'm homesick for all the beach towns I have known, Capri, Mallorca, the south of France, Venice, the Italian Riviera, South America."

"I understand that," he said. "I was homesick when I

first came to this country from Ireland."

"A year ago I was dancing on the beach, under palm trees. The music was wild, and the waves washed our feet while we danced."

"Yes, I know. I was once a bodyguard for a rich man. Everybody sat in the port cafes at night. It was like the Fourth of July, every night. Come along, I'll take you to my home. The wife and kids are asleep, but I can give you some aspirin."

She sat beside him. He continued to recall his life as a bodyguard, when he had travelled all around the world. He controlled the car without a dissonance.

"I hate this town," she said vehemently.

He had driven smoothly beside a neat white house. He said: "Wait here," and went into the house.

When he returned he was carrying a glass of water and two aspirin in the palm of his hand. Sabina's nerves began to untangle. She took the water and aspirin obediently.

He turned his powerful flashlight upon a bush in his garden and said: "Look at this!"

In the night she saw flowers of velvet with black hearts and gold eyes.

"What kind of a flower is that?" she asked, to please him.

"Roses of Sharon," he said reverently and with the purest of Irish accents. "They only grow in Ireland and on Long Island."

Sabina's rebellion was subsiding. She felt a tenderness for the roses of Sharon, for the policeman's protectiveness, for his effort to find a substitute for tropical flowers, a little beauty in the present night.

"I'll sleep now," she said. "You can drop me off at the Penny Cottage."

"Oh no," he said, sitting at the wheel. "We'll drive around by the sea until you're so sleepy you can't bear it anymore. You can't sleep you know, until you find something to be grateful for, you can never sleep when you're angry."

She could not hear very distinctly his long and rambling stories about his life as a bodyguard, except when he said: "There's two of you giving me trouble with homesickness today. The other was a young fellow in the English Air Corps. Aviator all through the war, seventeen when he volunteered. He's grounded now, and he can't take it. He's restless and keeps speeding and breaking traffic laws. The red lights drive him crazy. When I saw what it was, I stopped giving him tickets. He's used to airplanes. Being grounded is tough. I know how he feels."

She felt the mists of sleep rising from the ground, bearing the perfume of roses of Sharon; in the sky shone the eyes of the grounded aviator not yet accustomed to small scales, to shrunken spaces. There were other human beings attempting vast flights, with a kind policeman as tall as the crusaders watching over them with a glass of water and two aspirins; she could sleep now, she could sleep, she could find her bed with his flash-light shining on the keyhole, his car so smoothly so gently rolling away, his white hair saying sleep . . .

Sabina in the telephone booth. Alan has just said that he was unable to come that day. Sabina felt like sliding down on the floor and sobbing out the loneliness. She wanted to return to New York but he begged her to wait.

There were places which were like ancient tombs in which a day was a century of non-existence. He had said: "Surely you can wait another day. I'll be there tomorrow. Don't be unreasonable."

She could not explain that perfect lawns, costly churches, new cement and fresh paint can make a vast tomb without stone gods to admire, without jewels, or urns full of food for the dead, without hieroglyphs to decipher.

Telephone wires only carried literal messages, never the subterranean cries of distress, of desperation. Like telegrams they delivered only final and finite blows: arrivals, departures, births and deaths, but no room for fantasies such as: Long Island is a tomb, and one more day in it would bring on suffocation. Aspirin, Irish policeman, and roses of Sharon were too gentle a cure for suffocation.

Grounded. Just before she slid down to the floor, the bottom of the telephone cabin, the bottom of her loneliness, she saw the grounded aviator waiting to use the telephone. When she came out of the booth he looked distressed again as he seemed to be by everything that happened in time of peace. But he smiled when he recognized her saying: "You told me the way to the beach."

"You found it? You liked it?"

"A little flat for my taste. I like rocks and palm trees. Got used to them in India, during the war."

War as an abstraction had not yet penetrated Sabina's consciousness. She was like the communion seekers who received religion only in the form of a wafer on the tongue. War as a wafer placed on her tongue directly by the young aviator, came suddenly very close to her and she saw that if he shared with her his contempt for the placidities of peace it was only to take her straight into the infernal core of war. That was his world. When he said: "Get your bicycle then, and I'll show you a better beach further on . . ." it was not only to escape from fashionable reclining figures on the beach, from golf players and human barnacles glued to damp bar flanks, it was to bicycle into his inferno. As soon as they started to walk along the beach he began to talk:

"I've had five years of war as a rear gunner. Been to India a couple of years, been to North Africa, slept in the desert, crashed several times, made about one hundred missions, saw all kinds of things . . . Men dying, men yelling when they're trapped in burning planes. Their arms charred, their hands like claws of animals. The first time I was sent to the field after a crash . . . the smell of burning flesh. It's sweet and sickening, and it sticks to you for days. You can't wash it off. You can't get rid of it. It haunts you. We had good laughs, though, laughs all the time. We laughed plenty. We would steal prostitutes and push them into the beds of the men who didn't like women. We had drunks that lasted several days. I liked that life. India. I'd like to go back. This life here, what people talk about, what they do, think, bores me. I liked sleeping in the desert. I saw a black woman giving birth . . . she worked on the fields carrying dirt for a new airfield. She stopped carrying dirt to give birth under the wing of the plane, just like that, and then bound the kid in some rags and went back to work. Funny to see the big plane, so modern, and this half naked black woman giving birth and then continuing to carry dirt in pails for an airfield. You know, only two of us came back alive of the bunch I started with. We played pranks, though. My buddies always warned me: 'Don't get grounded; once you're grounded you're done for.' Well, they grounded me too. Too many rear gunners in the service. I didn't want to come home. What's civilian life? Good for old maids. It's a rut. It's drab. Look at this: the young girls giggle, giggle at nothing. The boys are after me. Nothing ever happens. They don't laugh hard and they don't yell. They don't get hurt, and they don't die, and they don't laugh either."

Always something in his eyes which she could not read, something he had seen but would not talk about.

"I like you because you hate this place, and because you don't giggle," he said taking her hand with gentleness.

They walked endlessly, tireslessly along the beach, until there were no more houses, no more cared-for gardens, no more people, until the beach became wild and showed no footsteps, until the debris from the sea lay "like a bombed museum," he said.

"I'm glad I found a woman who walks my stride as you do," he said. "And who hates what I hate."

As they bicycled homeward he looked elated, his smooth skin flushed with sun and pleasure. The slight trembling of his gestures had vanished.

The fireflies were so numerous they flew into their faces.

"In South America," said Sabina, "the women wear

fireflies in their hair, but fireflies stop shining when they go to sleep so now and then the women had to rub the fireflies to keep them awake."

John laughed.

At the door of the cottage where she stayed, he hesitated. He could see it was a rooming house in a private family's jurisdiction. She made no movement but fixed her enlarged, velvet-pupilled eyes on his and held them, as if to subdue the panic in them.

He said in a very low voice: "I wish I could stay with you." And then bent over to kiss her with a fraternal kiss, missing her mouth.

"You can if you wish."

"*They* will hear me."

"You know a great deal about war," said Sabina, "but I know a great deal about peace. There's a way you can come in and they will never hear you."

"Is that true?" But he was not reassured and she saw that he had merely shifted his mistrust of the critical family to mistrust of her knowledge of intrigue which made her a redoubtable opponent.

She was silent and made a gesture of abdication, starting to run towards the house. It was then he grasped her and kissed her almost desperately, digging his nervous, lithe fingers into her shoulders, into her hair, grasping her hair as if he were drowning to hold her head against his as if she might escape his grasp.

"Let me come in with you."

"Then take off your shoes," she whispered.

He followed her.

"My room is on the first floor. Keep in step with me as

we go up the stairs; they creak. But it will sound like one person."

He smiled.

When they reached her room, and she closed the door, he examined his surroundings as if to assure himself he had not fallen into an enemy trap.

His caresses were so delicate that they were almost like a teasing, an evanescent challenge which she feared to respond to as it might vanish. His fingers teased her, and withdrew when they had aroused her, his mouth teased her and then eluded hers, his face and body came so near, espoused her every limb and then slid away into the darkness. He would seek every curve and nook he could exert the pressure of his warm slender body against and suddenly lie still, leaving her in suspense. When he took her mouth he moved away from her hands, when she answered the pressure of his thighs, he ceased to exert it. Nowhere would he allow a long enough fusion, but tasting every embrace, every area of her body and then deserting it, as if to ignite only and then elude the final welding. A teasing, warm, trembling, elusive short circuit of the senses as mobile and restless as he had been all day, and here at night, with the street lamp revealing their nudity but not his eyes, she was roused to an almost unbearable expectation of pleasure. He had made of her body a bush of roses of Sharon, exfoliating pollen, each prepared for delight.

So long delayed, so long teased that when possession came it avenged the waiting by a long, prolonged, deep thrusting ecstasy.

The trembling passed into her body, she had amalga-

83

mated his anxieties, she had absorbed his delicate skin, his dazzling eyes.

The moment of ecstasy had barely ended when he moved away and he murmured: Life is flying, flying.

"This is flying," said Sabina. But she saw his body lying there no longer throbbing, and knew she was alone in her feeling, that this moment contained all the speed, all the altitude, all the space she wanted.

Almost immediately he began to talk in the dark, about burning planes, about going out to find the fragments of the living ones, to check on the dead.

"Some die silent," he said. "You know by the look in their eyes that they are going to die. Some die yelling, and you have to turn your face away and not look into their eyes. When I was being trained, you know, the first thing they told me: 'Never look into a dying man's eyes'."

"But you did," said Sabina.

"No, I didn't, I didn't."

"But I know you did. I can see it in your eyes; you did look into dying men's eyes, the first time perhaps . . ."

She could see him so clearly, at seventeen, not yet a man, with the delicate skin of a girl, the finely carved features, the small straight nose, the mouth of a woman, a shy laugh, something very tender about the whole face and body, looking into the eyes of the dying.

"The man who trained me said: 'Never look into the eyes of the dying or you'll go mad'. Do you think I'm mad? Is that what you mean?"

"You're not mad. You're very hurt, and very frightened, and very desperate, and you feel you have no right to live, to enjoy, because your friends are dead or dying, or flying still. Isn't that it?"

"I wish I were there now, drinking with them, flying, seeing new countries, new faces, sleeping in the desert, feeling you may die any moment and so you must drink fast, and fight hard, and laugh hard. I wish I were there now, instead of here, being bad."

"Being bad?"

"This is being bad, isn't it? You can't say it isn't, can you?"

He slipped out of bed and dressed. His words had destroyed her elation. She covered herself up to her chin with the sheet and lay silent.

When he was ready, before he gathered up his shoes, he bent over her, and in the voice of a tender young man playing at being a father he said: "Would you like me to tuck you in before I leave?"

"Yes, yes," said Sabina, her distress melting, "yes," she said with gratitude not for the gesture of protectiveness, but because if he considered her bad in his own vision, he would not have tucked her in. *One does not tuck in a bad woman.* And surely this gesture meant that perhaps he would see her again.

He tucked her in gently and with all the neatness of a flyer's training, using the deftness of long experience with camping. She lay back accepting this, but what he tucked in so gently was not a night of pleasure, a body satiated, but a body in which he had injected the poison which was killing him, the madness of hunger, guilt and death by proxy which tormented him. He had injected into her body his own venomous guilt for living and desiring. He had mingled poison with every drop of

85

pleasure, a drop of poison in every kiss, every thrust of sensual pleasure the thrust of a knife killing what he desired, killing with guilt.

The following day Alan arrived, his equable smile and equable temper unchanged. His vision of Sabina unchanged. Sabina had hoped he would exorcise the obsession which had enslaved her the night before, but he was too removed from her chaotic despair, and his extended hand, his extended love was unequal to the power of what was dragging her down.

The sharp, the intense moment of pleasure which had taken possession of her body, and the sharp intense poison amalgamated with it.

She wanted to rescue John from a distortion she knew led to madness. She wanted to prove to him that his guilt was a distortion, that his vision of her and desire as bad, and of his hunger as bad, was a sickness.

The panic, the hunger and terror of his eyes had passed into her. She wished she had never looked into his eyes. She felt a desperate need to abolish his guilt, the need of rescuing him because for a reason she could not fathom, she had sunk with him into the guilt; she had to rescue him and herself. He had poisoned her, transmitted his doom to her. She would go mad with him if she did not rescue him, and alter his vision.

If he had not tucked her in she might have rebelled against him, hated him, hated his blindness. But this act of tenderness had abolished all defenses: he was blind in error, frightened and tender, cruel and lost, and she was all these with him, by him, through him.

She could not even mock at his obsession with flying. His airplanes were not different from her relationships, by which she sought other lands, strange faces, forgetfulness, the unfamiliar, the fantasy and the fairytale.

87

She could not mock his rebellion against being grounded. She understood it, experienced it each time that, wounded, she flew back to Alan. If only he had not tucked her in, not as a bad woman, but as the child, the child he was in a terrifying, confusing world. If only he had left brutally, projecting his shame on her as so often woman bore the brunt of man's shame, shame thrown at her in place of stones, for seducing and tempting. Then she could have hated him, and forgotten him, but because he had tucked her in, he would come back. He had not thrown his shame at her, he had not said: "You're bad." One does not tuck in a bad woman.

But when they met accidentally, and he saw her walking beside Alan, at this moment, in the glance he threw at her, Sabina saw that he had succeeded in shifting the shame and that now what he felt was: *"You're* a bad woman," and that he would never come back to her. Only the poison remained, without hope of the counter-poison.

Alan left, and Sabina stayed with the hope of seeing John again. She sought him vainly at bars, restaurants, movie houses and at the beach. She inquired at the place where he rented his bicycle: they had not seen him but he still had his bicycle.

In desperation she inquired at the house where he rented a room. The room was paid for the next week, but he had not been there for three days and the woman was concerned because John's father had been telephoning every day.

The last time he had been seen was at the bar, with a group of strangers who had driven away with him.

Sabina felt she should return to New York and forget him, but his eager face and the distress in his eyes made this act seem one of desertion.

At other moments the pleasure he had given her ignited her body like flowing warm mercury darting through the veins. The memory of it flowed through the waves when she swam, and the waves seemed like his hands, or the form of his body in her hands.

She fled from the waves and his hands. But when she lay on the warm sand, it was his body again on which she lay; it was his dry skin and his swift elusive movements slipping through her fingers, shifting beneath her breasts. She fled from the sand of his caresses.

But when she bicycled home, she was racing him, she heard his merry challenges, faster — faster — faster in the wind, his face pursued her in flight or she pursued his face.

That night she raised her face to the moon, and the gesture awakened the pain, because to receive his kiss she had had to raise her face this way, but with the support of his two hands. Her mouth opened to receive his kiss once more but closed on emptiness. She almost shouted out with pain, shouted at the moon, the deaf, impassible goddess of desire shining down mockingly at an empty night, an empty bed.

She decided to pass once more by his house, although it was late, although she dreaded to see once more, the empty dead face of his window.

His window was alight and open!

Sabina stood under it and whispered his name. She was hidden by a bush. She dreaded that anyone else in the house should hear her. She dreaded the eyes of the world upon a woman standing under a young man's window.

"John! John!"

He leaned out of the window, his hair tousled, and even in the moonlight she could see his face was burning and his eyes hazy.

"Who's there?" he said, always with the tone of a man at war, fearing ambush.

"Sabina. I just wanted to know . . . are you all right?"

"Of course I'm all right. I was in the hospital."

"The hospital?"

"A bout of malaria, that's all."

"Malaria?"

"I get it, when I drink too much . . ."

"Will I see you tomorrow?"

He laughed softly: "My father is coming to stay with me."

"We won't be able to see each other then. I'd better return to New York."

"I'll call you when I get back."

"Will you come down and kiss me good-night?"

He hesitated: "They will hear me. They will tell my father."

"Good-bye, good-night . . ."

"Good-bye," he said, detached, cheerful.

But she could not leave Long Island. It was as if he had thrown a net around her by the pleasure she wanted again, by his creation of a Sabina she wanted to erase, by a poison he alone had the cure for, of a mutual guilt which only an act of love could transmute into something else than a one-night encounter with a stranger.

The moon mocked her as she walked back to her empty bed. The moon's wide grin which Sabina had never noticed before, never before its mockery of this quest of love which she influenced. *I understand his madness, why does he run away from me? I feel close to him, why does he not feel close to me, why doesn't he see the resemblance between us, between our madness. I want the impossible, I want to fly all the time, I destroy ordinary life, I run towards all the dangers of love as he ran towards all the dangers of war. He runs away, war is less terrifying to him than life . . .*

John and the moon left this madness unexorcised. No trace of it was revealed except when she was taunted:

"Aren't you interested in war news, don't you read the papers?"

"I *know* war, I know all about war."

"You never seem very close to it."

*(I slept with war, all night I slept with war once. I received deep war wounds into my body, as you never did, a feat of arms for which I will never be decorated!)*

In the multiple peregrinations of love, Sabina was quick to recognize the echoes of larger loves and desires. The large ones, particularly if they had not died a natural death, never died completely and left reverberations. Once interrupted, broken artificially, suffocated accidentally, they continued to exist in separate fragments and endless smaller echoes.

A vague physical resemblance, an almost similar mouth, a slightly similar voice, some particle of the character of Philip, or John, would emigrate to another, whom she recognized immediately in a crowd, at a party, by the erotic resonance it reawakened.

The echoes struck at first through the mysterious instrumentation of the senses which retained sensations as instruments retain a sound after being touched. The body remained vulnerable to certain repetitions long after the mind believed it had made a clear, a final severance.

A similar design of a mouth was sufficient to retransmit the interrupted current of sensations, to recreate a contact by way of the past receptivity, like a channel conducting perfectly only a part of the former ecstasy through the channel of the senses arousing vibrations and sensibilities formerly awakened by a total love or total desire for the entire personality.

The senses created river beds of responses formed in part from the sediments, the waste, the overflow from the original experience. A partial resemblance could stir what remained of the imperfectly rooted out love which had not died a natural death.

Whatever was torn out of the body, as out of the earth,

cut, violently uprooted, left such deceptive, such lively roots below the surface, all ready to bloom again under an artificial association, by a grafting of sensation, given new life through this graft of memory.

Out of the loss of John, Sabina retained such musical vibration below visibility which made her insensitive to men totally different from John and prepared her for a continuation of her interrupted desire for John.

When she saw the slender body of Donald, the same small nose, and head carried on a long-stemmed neck, the echo of the old violent emotions was strong enough to appear like a new desire.

She did not observe the differences, that Donald's skin was even more transparent, his hair silkier, that he did not spring, but glided, dragging his feet a little, that his voice was passive, indolent, slightly whining.

At first Sabina thought he was gently clowning by his parodies of women's feathery gestures, by a smile so deliberately seductive imitating the corolla's involutionary attractions.

She smiled indulgently when he lay down on the couch preparing such a floral arrangement of limbs, head, hands as to suggest a carnal banquet.

She laughed when he trailed his phrases like southern vines, or practised sudden exaggerated severities as children do when they play charades of the father's absurd arrogances, or the mother's hot-house exudations of charms.

When Sabina crossed the street, she nourished herself upon the gallant smile of the policeman who stopped the traffic for her, she culled the desire of the man who pushed the revolving door for her, she gathered the flash of adoration from the drug clerk: "Are you an actress?" She picked the bouquet of the shoe salesman trying on her shoes: "Are you a dancer?" As she sat in the bus she received the shafts of the sun as a personal, intimate visit. She felt a humorous connivance with the truck driver who had to pull the brakes violently before her impulsive passages, and who did so smiling because it was Sabina and they were glad to see her crossing their vision.

But she considered this feminine sustenance, like pollen. To her amazement, Donald, walking beside her, assumed these offerings were intended for him.

He passed what she believed to be from one mimicry to another: the pompous policeman, for which he filled his lungs with air, the sinuosities of the woman walking in front of them, for which he tangoed his hips.

Sabina was still laughing, wondering when the charades would end and the true Donald appear.

At this moment, in front of her at the restaurant table he was ordering with the exaggerated tyranny of the business executive, or he became prim with the salesgirl like a statesman with little time for charm. He ridiculed women in their cycles of periodic irrationality with an exact reproduction of whims, contrariness and commented on the foibles of fashion with a minute expertness Sabina lacked. He made her doubt her femininity by the greater miniature precision of his miniature interests. His love of small roses, of delicate jewelry seemed more feminine than her barbaric heavy necklaces, and her dislike of small flowers and nursery pastel blues.

At any moment, she believed, this playfulness would

cease, he would stand more erect and laugh with her at his own absurdities of dress, a shirt the color of her dress, a baroque watch, a woman's billfold, or a strand of hair dyed silver gray on his young luxuriant gold head.

But he continued to assume mock professions, to mock all of them. Above all he possessed a most elaborate encyclopedia of women's flaws. In this gallery he had most carefully avoided Joan of Arc and other women heroines, Madame Curie and other women of science, the Florence Nightingales, the Amelia Earharts, the women surgeons, the therapists, the artists, the collaborative wives. His wax figures of women were an endless concentrate of puerilities and treacheries.

"Where did you find all these repulsive women?" she asked one day, and then suddenly she could no longer laugh: caricature was a form of hatred.

In his gentleness lay his greatest treachery. His submission and gentleness lulled one while he collected material for future satires. His glance always came from below as if he were still looking up at the monumental figures of the parents from a child's vantage point. These immense tyrants could only be undermined with the subtlest parody: the mother, his mother, with her flurry of feathers and furs, always preoccupied with people of no importance, while he wept with loneliness and fought the incubus of nightmares alone.

She danced, she flirted, she whined, she whirled without devotion to his sorrows. Her caressing voice contained all the tormenting contradictions: the voice read him fairytales, and when he believed them and proceeded to pattern his life after them, this same voice gave an acid bath to all his wishes, longings, desires, and distributed words worse than a slap, a closed door or dessertless dinner.

And so today, with Sabina walking at his side believing she could destroy the corrosive mother by enacting her opposite, by full attentiveness to his secret wishes, not dancing with others, not flirting, never whining, focussing the full searchlight of her heart upon him, his eyes did not see her alone, but Sabina and a third woman forever present in a perpetual triangle, a menage-a-trois, in which the mother's figure often stood between them, intercepting the love Sabina desired, translating her messages to Donald in terms of repetitions of early disappointments, early treacheries, all the mother's sins against him.

He kneeled at her feet to relace the sandal which was undone, an act he performed with the delicacy not of an enamoured man, but of a child at a statue's feet, of a child intent on dressing woman, adorning her, but not for himself to claim. In performing these adulations he fulfilled a secret love for satin, for feathers, for trinkets, for adornment, and it was a caress not to Sabina's feet but to the periphery of all that he could caress without breaking the ultimate taboo: touching his mother's body.

To touch the silk which enwrapped her, the hair which stemmed from her, the flowers she wore.

Suddenly his face which had been bent over the task lifted to her with the expression of a blind man suddenly struck with vision. He explained: "Sabina! I felt a shock all through my body while I tied your sandals. It was like an electric shock."

And then as quickly, his face clouded with the subdued light of filtered emotions, and he returned to his neutral zone: some early, pre-man, fin-knowledge of woman, indirect, enveloping, but without any trace of a passage-way for erotic penetration. Brushings, silken radiations, homage of eyes alone, possession of a little finger, of a sleeve, never a full hand on a bare shoulder but a flight from touch, wavelets and rivulets of delicate incense, that was all that flowed from him to her.

The electric shock sank beneath his consciousness.

By touching her naked foot he had felt a unity resembling the first unity of the world, unity with nature, unity with the mother, early memories of an existence within the silk, warmth and effortlessness of a vast love. By touching her foot this empty desert which lay between him and other human beings, bristling with all the plants of defenses, the cactus varieties of emotional repellents, grown impenetrable between himself and other young men, even when they lay body to body, was annihilated. There were sensual acts in which he had not felt this sudden flowing together which had happened between her naked foot and his hands, between the heart of her and the core of himself. This heart of Sabina's which he imagined panoplied for refuge, and the core of himself which he had never felt before except as the crystal structure of his young man's body which he knew, in her presence, discovered to be soft and vulnerable.

He became aware of all his fragilities at once, his dependence, his need. Nearer she came, her face growing larger as she bent over him, her eyes brighter and warmer, nearer and nearer, melting his hostilities.

It was terribly sweet to be so naked in her presence. As in all the tropical climates of love, his skin softened, his hair felt silkier on his skin, his nerves untangled from their sharp wiry contortions. All the tensions of pretenses ceased. He felt himself growing smaller, back to his natural size, as in tales of magic, shrinking painlessly in order to enter this refuge of her heart, relinquishing the straining for maturity. But with this came all the corresponding moods of childhood: the agonized helplessness, the early defenselessness, the anguish at being at other's complete mercy.

It was necessary to arrest this invasion of her warmth which drugged his will, his uprightness in anger, to arrest this dissolution and flowing of one being into another which had already taken place once between his mother and then been violently shattered with the greatest shock and pain by her fickleness and frivolities. It was necessary to destroy this fluid warmth in which he felt himself absorbed, drowning as within the sea itself. Her body a chalice, a ciborium, a niche of shadows. Her gray cotton dress folded like an accordion around her feet, with the gold dust of secrecy between each rivulet of tissue, a journey of infinite detours in which his manhood would be trapped, captured.

He dropped her naked foot and rose stiffly. He took up where he had left off, took up the adolescent charades. His gentleness turned to limpness, the hand he extended to take the cape off her shoulders was as if severed from the rest of his body.

He took up following her, carrying her cape. He incensed her with words, he sat in the closest proximity, in her shadow, always near enough to bask in the warmth emanating from her body, always within reach of her hand, always with his shirt open at the throat in an oblique challenge to her hands, but the mouth in flight. Wearing around his waist the most unique belts so that her eyes would admire his waist, but the body in flight.

This design in space was a continuation of John's way of caressing her, the echo of his teasings. The tantalizing night spent in seeking the sources of pleasure but avoiding all possible dangers of welding their bodies into any semblance of marriage. It aroused in Sabina a similar suspense, all the erotic nerves awakened, throwing off futile, wasted sparks in space.

She saw his charades as a child's jealous imitations of a maturity he could not reach.

"You're sad, Sabina," he said, "come with me; I have things to show you." As if rising with her in his gyroscope of fantasy he took her to visit his collection of empty cages.

Cages crowded his room, some of bamboo from the Philipines, some in gilt, wrought with intricate designs from Persia, others peaked like tents, others like minature adobe houses, others like African huts of palm leaves. To some of the cages he himself had added turrets, towers from the Middle Ages, trapezes and baroque ladders, bathtubs made of mirrors, and a complete miniature jungle sufficient to give these prisons the illusion of freedom, to any wild or mechanical bird imprisoned in them.

"I prefer empty cages, Sabina, until I find a unique bird I once saw in my dreams."

Sabina placed the "Firebird" on the phonograph. The delicate footsteps of the Firebird were heard at first through infinite distance, each step rousing the phosphorescent sparks from the earth, each note a golden bugle to marshal delight. A jungle of dragon tails thrashing in erotic derisions, a brazier of flesh-smoking prayers, the multiple debris of the stained glass fountains of desire.

She lifted up the needle, cut the music harshly in mid-air.

"Why? Why? Why?" cried Donald, as if wounded.

Sabina had silenced the firebirds of desire, and now she extended her arms like widely extended wings, wings no longer orange, and Donald gave himself to their protective embrace. The Sabina he embraced was the one he needed, the dispenser of food, of fulfilled promises, of mendings and knitting, comforts and solaces, of blankets and reassurances, of heaters, medicines, potions and scaffolds.

"You're the firebird, Sabina, and that was why, until you came, all my cages were empty. It was you I wanted to capture." Then, with a soft, a defeated tenderness he lowered his eyelashes and added: "I know I have no way to keep you here, nothing to hold you here . . ."

Her breasts were no longer tipped with fire, they were the breasts of the mother, from which flowed nourishment. She deserted her other loves to fulfill Donald's needs. She felt: "I am a woman, I am warm, tender and nourishing. I am fecund and I am good."

Such serenity came with this state of being woman the mother! The humble, the menial task performing mother as she had known her in her own childhood.

When she found chaotic, hasty little notes from Donald telling her where he was and when he would return he always ended them: "You are wonderful. You are wonderful and good. You are generous and kind."

And these words calmed her anxiety more than sensual fulfillment had, calmed her fevers. She was shedding other Sabinas, believing she was shedding anxiety. Each day the colors of her dresses became more subdued, her walk less animal. It was as if in captivity, her brilliant plumage were losing its brilliance. She felt the metamorphosis. She knew she was moulting. But she did not know what she was losing in moulding herself to Donald's needs.

Once, climbing his stairs with a full market bag, she caught a dim silhouette of herself on a damp mirror, and was startled to see a strong resemblance to her mother.

What Donald had achieved by capturing her into his net of fantasy as the firebird (while in the absence of erotic climate he had subtly dulled her plumage) was not only to reach his own need's fulfillment but to enable her to rejoin her mother's image which was her image of goodness: her mother, dispenser of food, of solace, soft warm and fecund.

On the stained mirror stood the shadow and echo of her mother, carrying food. Wearing the neutral toned clothes of self-effacement, the faded garments of self-sacrifice, the external uniform of goodness.

In this realm, her mother's realm, she had found a moment's surcease from guilt.

Now she knew what she must say to Donald, to cure

his sense of smallness, and the smallness of what he had given her. She would say to him:

"Donald! Donald! You did give me something no one else could give me, you gave me my innocence! You helped me to find again the way to gain peace which I had learned as a child. When I was a child, only a little younger than you are now, after days of drugging myself with reading, with playing, with fantasies about people, with passionate friendships, with days spent hiding from my parents, with escapes, and all the activities which were termed bad, I found that by helping my mother, by cooking, mending, cleaning, scrubbing, and doing all the chores I most hated, I could appease this hungry and tyrannical conscience. It's no crime that you have remained a child, Donald. In some of the old fairytales, you know, many mature characters were shrunk back into midgets, as Alice was made small again to re-experience her childhood. It's the rest of us who are pretenders; we all pretend to be large and strong. You just are not able to pretend."

When she entered his room, she found a letter on her table.

Once she had said to him, when his moods had been too contradictory: "Adolescence is like cactus," and he had answered: "I'll write you a letter some day, with cactus milk!"

And here it was!

Letter to an actress: "From what you told me last night I see that you do not know your power. You are like a person who consumes herself in love and giving and does not know the miracles that are born of this. I felt this last night as I watched you act Cinderella, that you were whatever you acted, that you touched that point at which art and life meet and there is only BEING. I felt your hunger and your dreams, your pities and your desires at the same time as you awakened all of mine. I felt that you were not acting but dreaming; I felt that all of us who watched you could come out of the theatre and without transition could pass magically into another Ball, another snowstorm, another love, another dream. Before our very eyes you were being consumed by love and the dream of love. The burning of your eyes, of your gestures, a bonfire of faith and dissolution. You have the power. Never again use the word exhibitionism. Acting in you is a revelation. What the soul so often cannot say through the body because the body is not subtle enough, you can say. The body usually betrays the soul. You have the power of contagion, of transmitting emotion through the infinite shadings of your movements, the variations of your mouth's designs, the feathery palpitations of your eyelashes. And your voice, your voice more than any other voice linked to your breath, the breathlessness of feeling, so that you take one's breath away with you and carry one into the realm of breathlessness and silence. So much power you have, Sabina! The pain you felt afterwards was not the pain of failure or of exhibitionism, as you said, it must be the pain of having revealed so much that was of the spirit, like some great mystic revelation of compassion, and love and secret illusion, so that you expected this to have been communicated to others, and that they should respond as to a magic ritual. It must have been a shock when it did not happen to the audience, when they remained untransformed. But, to those who respond as I did, you appear as something beyond the actor who can transmit to others the power to feel, to believe. For me the miracle took place. You seemed the only one alive among the actors. What hurt you was that it was not acting, and that when it ended there was a break in the dream. You should have been protected from the violent transition. You should have been carried off the stage, so that you would not feel the change of level, from the stage to the street, and from the street to your home, and from there to another party, another love, another snowstorm, another pair of gold slippers.

It must take great courage to give to many what one often gives but to the loved one. A voice altered by love, desire, the smile of open naked tenderness. We are permitted to witness the exposure of all feelings, tenderness, anger, weakness, abandon, childishness, fear, all that we usually reveal only to the loved one. That is why we love the actress. They give us the intimate being who is only revealed in the act of love. We receive all the treasures, a caressing glance, an intimate gesture, the secret ranges of the voice. This openness, which is closed again as soon as we face a partial relationship, the one who understands only one part of us, is the miraculous openness which takes place in whole love. And so I witnessed on the stage, this mystery of total love which in my life is hidden from me. And now, Sabina, I cannot bear the little loves, and yet I cannot claim all of yours, and every day I see you now, immense, complete, and I but a fragment, wandering . . ."

Sabina touched the letter which rested on her breast,

the sharp corners of the pages hurting her a little ...
"What can I give you," he asked, "What have I to give
you?" he cried out in anguish, thinking this was the
reason why he had not seen her for three days, or heard
from her. Another time he had said playfully: "I can
only nibble at you." And had pressed his small, perfect
teeth into her shoulder.

The ascensions of the ballet dancers into space and
their return to the ground, brought before her eyes a
Japanese umbrella made of colored paper which she once
wore in her hair. It was lovely to see, so delicately made.
When it rained and others opened their umbrellas then
it was time for her to close hers.

But a high wind had torn it, and when she went into
Chinatown to buy another the woman who ran the shop
shouted violently: "It's made in Japan, throw it in the
gutter!"

Sabina had looked at the parasol, innocent and fragile,
made in a moment of peace by a workman dreaming of
peace, made like a flower, lighter than war and hatred.
She left the shop and looked down at the gutter and could
not bring herself to throw it. She folded it quietly, folded
tender gardens, the fragile structure of dream, a workman's dream of peace, innocent music, innocent workman whose hands had not made bullets. In time of war
hatred confused all the values, hatred fell upon cathe-
drals, paintings, music, rare books, children, the innocent
passersby.

She folded the letter, as she had folded the parasol,
out of sight of hatred and violence. She could not keep
pace with the angry pulse of the world. She was engaged

in a smaller cycle, the one opposite to war. There were truths women had been given to protect while the men went to war. When everything would be blown away, a paper parasol would raise its head among the debris, and man would be reminded of peace and tenderness.

Alan always believed he was giving Sabina pleasure when he took her to the theatre, and at first her face was always illumined with suspense and curiosity. But inevitably, she would grow restive and tumultuous, chaotic and disturbed; she would even weep quietly in the dark and disappear in between acts, so as not to expose a ravaged face.

"What is it, what is it?" repeated Alan patiently, suspecting her of envy or jealousy of the roles given to others. "You could be the most marvellous actress of our period if you wanted to give your whole life to it, but you know how you feel about discipline and monotony."

"It isn't that, no, it isn't that," and Sabina would say no more.

To whom could she explain that what she envied them was the ease with which they would step out of their roles, wash themselves of it after the play and return to their true selves. She would have wanted these metamorphoses of her personality to take place on the stage so that at a given signal she would know for certain they were ended and she might return to a permanent immutable Sabina.

But when she wished to end a role, to become herself again, the other felt immensely betrayed, and not only fought the alteration but became angered at her. Once a role was established in a relationship it was almost impossible to alter. And even if she succeeded, when the time came to return to the original Sabina, where was she? If she rebelled against her role towards Donald, if she turned on the Firebird record again, the drumming of the senses the tongues of fire and denied her mother within her, was she then returning to the true **Sabina**?

When she replaced the needle on the record and set off on her first assignation with desire was it not her father then walking within her, directing her steps? Her father who, having fed on her mother's artful cooking, having dressed in the shirt she had ironed, having kissed her unbeautiful forehead damp from ironing, having allowed her marred hands to tie his tie, proceeded to leave her mother and Sabina for his vainglorious walk down the streets of the neighborhood who knew him for his handsomeness and his wanderings?

How many times had a perfumed, a painted, a handsome woman stopped her on the street to kiss her, caress her long hair and say: "You're Sabina! You're his daughter! I know your father *so* well." It was not the words, it was the intimate glance, the boudoir tone of the voice which alarmed her. This knowledge of her father always brought to women's eyes a sparkle not there before, an intimation of secret pleasures. Even as a child Sabina could read their messages. Sabina was the daughter of delight born of his amorous genius and they caressed her as another manifestation of a ritual she sensed and from which her mother had been estranged forever.

"I knew your father so well!" Always the handsome women bending over her, hateful with perfume one could not resist smelling, with starched petticoats and provocative ankles. For all these humiliations she would have wanted to punish her father, for all his desecrations of multiple summer evenings of wanderings which gave these women the right to admire her as another of his women. She was also angry at her mother for not being angry, for preparing and dressing him for these intruders.

Was it Sabina now rushing into her own rituals of pleasure, or was it her father within her, his blood guiding her into amorousness, dictating her intrigues, he who was inexorably woven with her by threads of inheritance she could never separate again to know which one was Sabina, which one her father whose role she had assumed by alchemy of mimetic love.

Where was Sabina?

She looked at the sky and she saw the face of John speeding in the pursued clouds, his charm fading like smoke from celestial pyres; she saw the soft night glow of Mambo's eyes saying: "You don't love me," while bearing down on her; and Philip laughing a conqueror's laugh, bearing down on her and his charm vanishing too before the thoughtful, withdrawn face of Alan. The entire sky a warm blanket of eyes and mouths shining down on her, the air full of voices now raucous from the sensual spasm, now gentle with gratitude, now doubtful, and she was afraid because there was no Sabina, not ONE, but a multitude of Sabinas lying down yielding and being dismembered, constellating in all directions and breaking. A small Sabina who felt weak at the center carried on a giant wave of dispersion. She looked at the sky arched overhead but it was not a protective sky, not a cathedral vault, not a haven; it was a limitless vastness to which she could not cling, and she was weeping: "Someone hold me — hold me, so I will not continue to race from one love to another dispersing me, disrupting me ... *Hold me to one ...*"

Leaning out of the window at dawn, pressing her breasts upon the window sill, she still looked out of the window hoping to see what she had failed to possess. She looked at the ending nights and the passersby with the keen alertness of the voyager who can never reach termination as ordinary people reach peaceful terminals at the end of each day, accepting pauses, deserts, havens, as she could not accept them.

Sabina felt lost.

The wild compass whose fluctuations she had always obeyed, making for tumult and motion in place of direction, was suddenly fractured so that she no longer knew even the relief of ebbs and flows and dispersions.

She felt lost. The dispersion had become too vast, too extended. A shaft of pain cut through the nebulous pattern, Sabina had always moved so fast that all pain had passed swiftly as through a sieve leaving a sorrow like children's sorrows, soon forgotten, soon replaced by another interest. She had never known a pause.

Her cape which was more than a cape, which was a sail, which was the feelings she threw to the four winds to be swelled and swept by the wind in motion, lay becalmed.

Her dress was becalmed.

It was as if now she were nothing that the wind could catch, swell and propel.

For Sabina, to be becalmed meant to die.

Anxiety had entered her body and refused to run through it. The silvery holes of her sieve against sorrow granted her at birth, had clogged. Now the pain had lodged itself inside of her, inescapable.

She had lost herself somewhere along the frontier between her inventions, her stories, her fantasies and her true self. The boundaries had become effaced, the tracks lost; she had walked into pure chaos, and not a chaos which carried her like the galloping of romantic riders in operas and legends, but which suddenly revealed the stage props: A papier-mâché horse.

She had lost her sails, her cape, her horse, her seven-league boots, and all of them at once. She was stranded in the semi-darkness of a winter evening.

Then, as if all the energy and warmth had been drawn inward for the first time, killing the external body, blurring the eyes, dulling the ears, thickening the palate and tongue, slowing the movements of the body, she felt intensely cold and shivered with the same tremor as leaves, feeling for the first time some withered leaves of her being detaching themselves from her body.

As she entered Mambo's Night Club she noticed new paintings on the walls and for a moment imagined herself back in Paris, seven years back, when she had first met Jay in Montparnasse.

She recognized his paintings instantly.

It was now as before in Paris exhibits, all the methods of scientific splitting of the atom applied to the body, and to the emotions. His figures exploded and constellated into fragments, like spilled puzzles, each piece having flown far enough away to seem irretrievable and yet not far enough to be dissociated. One could, with an effort of the imagination reconstruct a human figure completely from these fragments kept from total annihilation in space by an invisible tension. By one effort of contraction at the core they might still amalgamate to form the body of a woman.

No change in Jay's painting, but a change in Sabina who understood for the first time what they meant. She could see at this moment on the wall *an exact portrait of herself as she felt inside.*

Had he painted Sabina, or something happening to all of them as it was happening in chemistry, in science?

They had found all the corrosive acids, all the disintegrations, all the alchemies of separateness.

But when the painter exposed what took place inside the body and emotions of man, they starved him, or gave him Fifth Avenue shop windows to do, where Paris La Nuit in the background allowed fashions to display hats and shoes and handbags and waists floating in mid-air, and waiting to be assembled on one complete woman.

She stood before the paintings and she now could see the very minute fragments of her acts which she had believed unimportant causing minute incisions, erosions of the personality. A small act, a kiss given at a party to a young man who benefitted from his resemblance to a lost John, a hand abandoned in a taxi to a man not desired but because the other woman's hand had been claimed and Sabina could not bear to have her hand lie unclaimed on her lap: it seemed an affront to her powers of seduction. A word of praise about a painting she had not liked but uttered out of fear that the painter would say: "Oh, Sabina . . . Sabina doesn't understand painting."

All the small insincerities had seeped like invisible rivulets of acid and caused profound damages, the erosions had sent each fragment of Sabina rotating like separate pieces of colliding planets, into other spheres, yet not powerful enough to fly into space like a bird, not organic enough to become another life, to rotate on its own core.

Jay's painting was a dance of fragments to the rhythm of debris. It was also a portrait of the present Sabina.

And all her seeking of fire to weld these fragments together, seeking in the furnace of delight a welding of

113

fragments into one total love, one total woman, had failed!

When she turned away from the paintings she saw Jay sitting at one of the tables, his face more than ever before resembling Lao Tze. His half bald head rimmed now with frosty white hair, his half-closed, narrow, small eyes laughing.

Someone standing between Sabina and Jay leaned over to compliment him on his Fifth Avenue windows. Jay laughed merrily and said: "I have the power to stun them, and while they are stunned by modern art the advertisers can do their poisonous jobs."

He waved at Sabina to sit down with him.

"You've been watching my atomic pile in which men and women are bombarded to find the mysterious source of power in them, a new source of strength." He talked to her as if no years had intervened between their last meeting at a café in Paris. He was always continuing the same conversation begun no one knew when, perhaps in Brooklyn where he had been born, everywhere and anywhere until he had reached the country of cafes where he found an audience, so that he could paint and talk perpetually in one long chain of dissertations.

"Have you found your power, your new strength," asked Sabina, "I haven't."

"I haven't either," said Jay, with mock contrition. "I've just come home, because of the war. They asked us to leave, whoever couldn't be drafted was only one more mouth to feed for France. The consulate sent us a messenger: 'Let all the useless ones leave Paris.' In one day all the artists deserted, as if the plague had come. I never knew the artists occupied so much space! We the international artists were faced with either hunger or concentration camps. Do you remember Hans, Sabina? They wanted to send him back to Germany. A minor Paul Klee, that's true, but still deserving a better fate. And Suzanne was sent back to Spain, she had no papers, her Hungarian husband with the polio was put in a camp. Remember the corner of Montparnasse and Raspail where we all stood for hours saying good-night? Because of the blackouts you'd have no time to say goodnight, you'd be lost as soon as you were out of the café, you'd vanish in the black night. Innocence was gone from all our acts. Our habitual state of rebellion became a serious political crime. Djuna's house boat was drafted for the transportation of coal. Everything could undergo conversion except the artists. How can you convert disorganizers of past and present order, the chronic dissenters, those dispossessed of the present anyway, the atomb bomb throwers of the mind, of the emotions, seeking to generate new forces and a new order of mind out of continuous upheavals?"

As he looked at Sabina his eyes seemed to say that she had not changed, that she was still for him, the very symbol of this fever and restlessness and upheavals and anarchy in life which he had applauded in Paris seven years ago.

At this moment another personage sat down next to Jay. "Meet Cold Cuts, Sabina. Cold Cuts is our best friend here. When people get transplanted, it's exactly like plants; at first there's a wilting, a withering; some die of it. We're all at the critical stage, suffering from a change of soil. Cold Cuts works at the morgue. His constant familiarity with suicides and terrifying description of them keeps us from committing it. He speaks sixteen languages and thus he's the only one who can talk to all the artists, at least early in the evening. Later he'll be drunk in extremis and will only be able to speak the esperanto of alcoholics, which is a language full of stutterings from the geological layers of our animal ancestors."

Satisfied with this introduction, Cold Cuts left the table and busied himself with the microphone. But Jay was wrong, although it was only nine o'clock, Cold Cuts was already in difficulties with the microphone. He was struggling to maintain an upright relationship, but the microphone would yield, bend, sway under his embrace like a flexible young reed. In his desperate embraces, it seemed as if the instrument and Cold Cuts would finally lie on the floor entangled like uncontrollable lovers.

When a momentary equilibrium was established, Cold Cuts became voluble and sang in sixteen various languages (including alcoholic esperanto) becoming in quick successions, a French streetsinger, a German opera singer, a Viennese organ grinder singer, etc.

Then he returned to sit with Jay and Sabina.

"Tonight Mambo cut off my food supply earlier than usual. Why, do you think? I shouldn't be so loyal to him. But he doesn't want me to lose my job. At midnight I must be fit to receive the dead politely. I mustn't stutter or bungle anything. The dead are sensitive. Oh, I have a perfect suicide to report to the exiles: a European singer who was spoiled and pampered in her own country. She strangled herself with all her colored scarves tied together. Do you think she wanted to imitate the death of Isadora Duncan?"

"I don't believe that," said Jay. "I can reconstruct the scene. She was a failure as a singer here. Her present life was gray, she was forgotten and not young enough to conquer a second time perhaps . . . She opened her trunk full of programs of past triumphs, full of newspaper clippings praising her voice and her beauty, full of dried flowers which had been given to her, full of love letters grown yellow, full of colored scarves which brought back the perfumes and the colors of her past successes, and by contrast her life today became unbearable."

"You're absolutely right," said Cold Cuts. "I'm sure that's the way it happened. She hung herself on the umbilical cord of the past." He sputtered as if all the alcohol he contained had begun to bubble within him and said to Sabina: "Do you know why I'm so loyal to Mambo? I'll tell you. In my profession people would rather forget me. No one wants to be reminded of death. Maybe they don't want to ignore *me*, but the company I keep. Now I don't mind this the rest of the year, but I do mind it at Christmas. Christmas comes and I'm the only one who never gets a Christmas card. And that's the one thing about my work at the Morgue which I can't stand. So a few days before Christmas I said to Mambo: 'Be sure and send me a Christmas card. I've got to receive at least *one* Christmas card. I've got to feel one person at least thinks of me at Christmas time, as if I were a human being like any other.' But you know Mambo — He promised, he smiled, and then once he starts drumming it's like a jag of some kind, and you can't sober him up.

117

I couldn't sleep for a week thinking he might forget and how I would feel on Christmas day to be forgotten *as if I were dead* . . . Well, he didn't forget."

Then with unexpected swiftness, he pulled an automobile horn out of his pocket, affixed it to his buttonhole and pressed it with the exuberance of a woman squeezing perfume from an atomizer and said: "Listen to the language of the future. The word will disappear altogether and that is how human beings will talk to each other!"

And bowing with infinite control of the raging waters of alcohol which were pressing against the dam of his politeness, Cold Cuts prepared to leave for his duties at the morgue.

Mambo began his drumming and Sabina began to look feverish and trapped as she had looked the first time Jay had seen her.

*Dressed in red and silver, she evoked the sounds and imagery of fire engines as they tore through the streets of New York, alarming the heart with the violent accelerations of catastrophies.*

*All dressed in red and silver, she evoked the tearing red and silver siren cutting a pathway through the flesh.*

*The first time he had looked at her he had felt: "Everything will burn!"*

*Out of the red and silver and the long cry of alarm to the poet who survives (even if secretly and invisibly) in every human being as the child survives in him (denied and disguised) to this poet she threw an unexpected challenge, a ladder in the middle of the city and ordained: "Climb!"*

*As she appeared all orderly alignment of the city gave way before this ladder one was invited to climb, standing straight in space like the ladder of Baron Munchausen which led to the sky.*

*Only her ladders led to fire.*

Jay laughed and shook his head from side to side, at the persistance of the image he had of Sabina. After seven years she *still had not learned to sit still. She talked profusely and continuously with a feverish breathlessness like one in fear of silence. She sat as if she could not bear to sit for long and when she rose to buy cigarettes she was equally eager to return to her seat. Impatient, alert, watchful, as if in dread of being attacked, restless and keen. She drank hurriedly, she smiled so swiftly that he was never certain it had been a smile, she listened only partially to what was being said to her, and even when someone in the bar leaned over and shouted out her name in her direction she did not respond at first, as if it were not her own.*

*Her way of looking at the door of the bar as if expecting the proper moment to make her escape, her erratic and sudden gestures, her sudden sulky silences, she behaved like someone who had all the symptoms of guilt.*

Above the iridescence of the candles, above the mists of cigarette smoke and the echoes of the cajoling blues, Sabina was aware that Jay was meditating on her. But it would be too dangerous to question him; he was a satirist, and all she would obtain from him at this moment was a caricature, which she could not take lightly or dismiss, and which would, in her present mood, add heavily to the weights pulling her downward.

Whenever Jay shook his head kindly, with the slow heavy playfulness of a bear, he was about to say something devastating which he called his brutal honesty. And Sabina would not challenge this. So she began a swift, spiralling, circuitous story about a party at which indistinct incidents had taken place, hazy scenes from which no one could distinguish the heroine or the victim. By the time Jay had felt he recognized the place (Montparnasse, seven years ago, a party at which Sabina had actually been jealous of the strong bond between Jay and Lillian which she was seeking to break) Sabina was already gone from there, and talking as in a broken dream, with spaces, reversals, retractions and galloping fantasies.

*She was now in Morocco, visiting the Arabian baths with the native women, sharing their pumice stone, and learning from the prostitutes how to paint her eyes with khol from the market place.*

"It's coal dust," explained Sabina, "and you place it right inside of the eyes. It smarts at first, and it makes you cry, but that spreads it out on the edge of the eyelids and that is how they get that shiny, coal black rim around the eyes."

"Didn't you get an infection?" asked Jay.

"Oh, no, the prostitutes are very careful to have the kohl blessed at the mosque."

Everyone laughed at this, Mambo who had been standing near, Jay and two indistinct personages who had been sitting at the next table but who had been sliding their chairs to listen to Sabina. Sabina did not laugh; she was invaded by another memory of Morocco; Jay could see the images passing through her eyes like a film being censored. He knew she was busy eliminating other stories she was about to tell; she might even be regretting the story about the bath, and now it was as if all she had said had been written on a huge blackboard and she took a sponge and effaced it all by adding: "Actually, this did not happen to me. It was told to me by someone who went to Morocco," and before anyone could ask: "Do you mean that you never went to Morocco at all?" she continued to confuse the threads by adding that this was a story she had read somewhere or heard at a bar, and as soon as she had erased in the minds of her listeners any facts which could be directly attributed to her own responsibility, she began another story . . .

The faces and the figures of her personages appeared only half drawn, and when Jay had barely begun to reconstruct the missing fragment (when she told about the man who was polishing his own telescope glass she did not want to say too much for fear Jay would recognize Philip whom he had known in Vienna and whom they all called playfully in Paris: "Vienna-as-it-was-before-the-war") when Sabina would interpose another face and figure as one does in dreams, and when Jay had laboriously decided she was talking about Philip (with whom he was sure now she had had an affair) it turned out that she was no longer talking about a man polishing a telescope glass with the umbrella hung up in the middle of the room above his work, but about a woman who had continued to play the harp at a concert in Mexico City during the revolution when someone had shot at the lights of the concert hall, and she had felt that if she continued to play she would prevent a panic, and as Jay knew this story had

121

been told of Lillian, and that it was not a harpist but as a pianist that Lillian had continued to play, Sabina became aware that she did not want to remind Jay about Lillian as it would be painful to him, and that the memory of her desertion of him was to some extent an event for which Sabina's seduction of Jay in Paris had been in part responsible, and so she quickly reversed her story and it was Jay who wondered whether he was not hearing right, whether perhaps he had been drinking too much and had imagined she was talking about Lillian, because actually at this very moment she was talking about a young man, an aviator, who had been told not to look into the eyes of the dead.

Jay could not retain any sequence of the people she had loved, hated, escaped from, anymore than he could keep track of her very personal appearance as she herself would say: "At that time I was a blond, and I wore my hair very short," or, "this was before I was married when I was only nineteen" (and once she had told him she had been married at the age of eighteen). Impossible to know who she had betrayed, forgotten, married, deserted, or clung to. It was like her profession. The first time he had questioned her she had answered immediately: "I am an actress." But when he pressed her he could not find in what play she had acted, whether she had been a success or a failure, whether, perhaps, (as he decided later) she had merely *wished* to be an actress but had never worked persistently enough, seriously enough except in the way she was working now, changing personalities with such rapidity that Jay was reminded of a kaleidoscope.

He sought to capture the recurrence of certain words

in her talk, thinking they might be used as keys, but if the word "actress", "miraculous", "travel", "wandering", "relationship" did occur frequently, it remained impossible whether or not she used them in their literal sense or symbolically, for they were the same to her. He had heard her say once: "When you are hurt you travel as far as you can from the place of the hurt," and when he examined her meaning found she was referring to a change of quarters within fifty blocks in the city of New York.

She was compelled by a confessional fever which forced her into lifting the veil slightly, only a corner of it, and then frightened when anyone listened too attentively especially Jay whom she did not trust, whom she knew found the truth only in the sense of exposure of the flaws, the weaknesses, the foibles.

As soon as Jay listened too attentively, she took a giant sponge and erased all she had said by an absolute denial as if this confusion were in itself a mantle of protection.

At first she beckoned and lured one into her world then she blurred the passageways, confused all the images *as if to elude detection.*

"False mysteries," said Jay savagely, baffled and irritated by her elusiveness. "But what is she hiding behind these false mysteries?"

Her behaviour always aroused in him (in the kind of mind he had with an obsession for truth, for revelation, for openness, brutal exposure) a desire which resembled the desire of a man to violate a woman who resists him, to violate a virginity which creates a barrier to his possession. Sabina always incited him to a violent desire to rip

123

all her pretenses, her veils, and to discover the core of her self which, by this perpetual change of face and mobility escaped all detection.

How right he had been to paint Sabina always as *a mandrake with fleshly roots, bearing a solitary purple flower in a purple-bell-shaped corolla of narcotic flesh. How right he had been to paint her born with red-gold eyes always burning as from caverns, from behind trees, as one of the luxuriant women, a tropical growth, excommunicated from the bread line as too rich a substance for every day living, placing her there merely as a denizen of the world of fire, and was content with her intermittent, parabolic appearances.*

"Sabina, do you remember our elevator ride in Paris?"

"Yes, I do remember."

"We had no place to go. We wandered through the streets. I remember it was your idea to take an elevator."

(We were ravenous for each other, I remember, Sabina. We got into an elevator and I began to kiss her. First floor. Second floor. I couldn't let go of her. Third floor, and when the elevator came to a standstill it was too late . . . I couldn't stop, I couldn't let go of her if all Paris had been watching us. She pressed the button wildly, and we went on kissing as the elevator came down. When we got to the bottom it was worse, so she pressed the button again, and we went up and down, up and down, while people kept trying to stop it and get on . . .)

Jay laughed uncontrollably at the memory, at Sabina's audacity. At that moment Sabina had been stripped of all mystery and Jay had tasted what the mystery contained: the most ardent frenzy of desire.

124

The dawn appearing weakly at the door silenced them. The music had ceased long ago and they had not noticed. They had continued their own drumming in talk.

Sabina tightened her cape around her shoulders as if daylight were the greatest enemy of all. To the dawn she would not even address a feverish speech. She stared at it angrily, and left the bar.

There is no bleaker moment in the life of the city than that one which crosses the boundary lines between those who have not slept all night and those who are going to work. It was for Sabina as if two races of men and women lived on earth, the night people and the day people, never meeting face to face except at this moment. Whatever Sabina had worn which seemed to glitter during the night, lost its colors in the dawn. The determined expressions of those going to work appeared to her like a reproach. Her fatigue was not like theirs. Hers marked her face like a long fever, left purple shadows under her eyes. She wanted to conceal her face from them. She hung her head so that her hair would partly cover it.

The mood of lostness persisted. For the first time she felt she could not go to Alan. She carried too great a weight of untold stories, too heavy a weight of memories, she was followed by too many ghosts of personages unsolved, of experiences not yet understood, of blows and humiliations not yet dissolved. She might return and plead extreme tiredness, and fall asleep, but her sleep would be restive, and she might talk in her dreams.

This time Alan would not have the power to exorcise her mood. Nor could she tell him about the event which most tormented her: the man she had first seen some months ago from the window of her hotel room, standing under her very window reading a newspaper, as if waiting for her to come out. Once more she had seen him on her way to visit Philip. She had encountered him in the subway station, and he had let several subway cars pass by in order to take the one she was taking.

It was not a flirtation. He made no effort to speak to

her. He seemed engaged in an impersonal observation of her. In Mambo's Night Club he had sat a few tables away and he was writing in a note book.

This was the way criminals were shadowed, just before being caught. Was he a detective? What did he suspect her of? Would he report to Alan? Or to her parents? Or would he take his notes downtown to all the awesome buildings in which they carried on investigations of one kind or another, and would she receive one day a notice asking her to leave the United States and return to her place of birth, Hungary, because the life of Ninon de l'Enclos, or Madame Bovary was not permitted by the law?

If she told Alan that she had been followed by a man, Alan would smile and say: "Why, of course, this isn't the first time, is it? That's the penalty you pay for being a beautiful woman. You wouldn't want it not to happen, would you?"

For the first time, on this bleak early morning walk through New York streets not yet cleaned of the night people's cigarette butts and empty liquor bottles, she understood Duchamp's painting of a Nude Descending a Staircase. Eight or ten outlines of the same woman, like many multiple exposures of a woman's personality, neatly divided into many layers, walking down the stairs in unison.

If she went to Alan now it would be like detaching one of these cut-outs of a woman, and forcing it to walk separately from the rest, but once detached from the unison, it would reveal that it was a mere outline of a woman, the figure design as the eye could see it, but empty of substance, this substance having evaporated through the spaces between each layer of the personality. A divided woman indeed, a woman divided into numberless silhouettes, and she could see this apparent form of Sabina leaving a desperate and a lonely one walking the streets in quest of hot coffee, being greeted by Alan as a transparently innocent young girl he had married ten years before and sworn to cherish, as he had, only he had continued to cherish the same young girl he had married, the first exposure of Sabina, the first image delivered into his hands, the first dimension, of this elaborated, complex and extended series of Sabinas which had been born later and which she had not been able to give him. Each year, just as a tree puts forth a new ring of growth, she should have been able to say: "Alan, here is a new version of Sabina, add it to the rest, fuse them well, hold on to them when you embrace her, hold them all at once in your arm, or else, divided, separated, each image will live a life of its own, and it will not be one but six, or seven, or eight Sabinas who will walk sometimes in unison, by a great effort of synthesis, sometimes separately, one of them following a deep drumming into forests of black hair and luxurious mouths, another visiting Vienna-as-it-was-before-the-war, and still another lying beside an insane young man, and still another opening maternal arms to a trembling frightened Donald. Was this the crime to have sought to marry each Sabina to another mate, to match each one in turn by a different life?

Oh, she was tired, but it was not from loss of sleep, or from talking too much in a smoke-filled room, or from eluding Jay's caricatures, or Mambo's reproaches, or

Philip's distrust of her, or because Donald by his behavior so much like a child had made her feel that her thirty years were a grandmother's age. She was tired of pulling these disparate fragments together. She understood Jay's paintings, too. It was perhaps at such a moment of isolation that Madame Bovary had taken the poison. It was the moment when the hidden life is in danger of being exposed, and no woman could bear the condemnation.

But why should she fear exposure? At this moment Alan was deeply asleep, or quietly reading if he were not asleep.

Was it merely this figure of a lie detector dogging her steps which caused her so acute an anxiety?

Guilt is the one burden human beings cannot bear alone.

After taking a cup of coffee, she went to the hotel where they knew her already, took a sleeping pill, and took refuge in sleep.

When she awakened at ten o'clock that night she could hear from her hotel room, the music from Mambo's Night Club across the street.

She needed a confessor! Would she find it there, in the world of the artists? All over the world they had their meeting places, their affiliations, their rules of membership, their kingdoms, their chiefs, their secret channels of communication. They established common beliefs in certain painters, certain musicians, certain writers. They were the misplaced persons, too, unwanted at home, usually, or repudiated by their families. But they established new families, their own religions, their own doctors, their own communities.

129

She remembered someone asking Jay: "Can I be admitted if I show proofs of excellent taste?"

"That is not enough," said Jay. "Are you also willing to become an exile? Or a scapegoat? We are the notorious scapegoats, for living as others live only in their dreams at night, for confessing openly what others only confess to doctors under guarantee of professional secret. We are also underpaid: people feel that we are in love with our work, and that one should not be paid for doing what you most love to do."

In this world they had criminals too. Gangsters in the world of art, who produced corrosive works born of hatred, who killed and poisoned with their art. You can kill with a painting or a book too.

Was Sabina one of them? What had she destroyed?

She entered Mambo's Night Club. The artificial palm trees seemed less green, the drums less violent. The floor, doors, walls were slightly askew with age.

Djuna arrived at the same moment, her black rehearsal tights showing under her raincoat, her hair bound in a ribbon like a school-girl.

When such magical entrances and exits take place in a ballet, when the dancers vanish behind columns or dense hills of shadows, no one asks them for passports or identifications. Djuna arrived as a true dancer does, walking as naturally from her ballet bar work a few floors above the night club as she had in Paris when she studied with the Opera ballet dancers. Sabina was not surprised to see her. But what she remembered of her was not so much her skill in dancing, her smooth dancer's legs, tense, but the skill of her compassion, as if she exercised everyday on an invisible bar of pain, her understanding as well as her body.

Djuna would know who had stolen, who had betrayed, and what had been stolen, what had been betrayed. And Sabina might cease falling — falling from all her incandescent trapezes, from all her ladders to fire.

They were all brothers and sisters, moving on the revolving stages of the unconscious, never intentionally mystifying others as much as themselves, caught in a ballet of errors and impersonations, but Djuna could distinguish between illusion and living and loving. She could detect the shadow of a crime which others could not bring to trial. She would know the identity of the criminal.

Sabina had only to wait now.

The drums ceased to play as if they were muffled by several forests of intricate impenetrable vegetation. Sabina's anxiety had ceased to beat against her temples, and deafen her to outer sounds. Rhythm was restored to her blood, and her hands lay still on her lap.

While she waited for Djuna to be free she thought about the lie detector who had been watching her actions. He was there in the café again, sitting alone, and writing in a note book. She prepared herself mentally for the interview.

She leaned over and called him: "How do you do? Have you come to arrest me?"

He closed his note book, walked over to her table, sat down beside her. She said: *I knew it would happen, but not quite so soon. Sit down. I know exactly what you think of me. You are saying to yourself: here is the* notorious impostor, the international spy in the house of love. (*Or should I specify: in the house of many loves?*) I must warn you, you must handle me delicately: I am covered with a mantle of iridescence as easily destroyed as a dust flower, and although I am quite willing to be arrested, if you handle me roughly you will lose much of the evidence. I don't want you to taint that fragile coat of astonishing colors created by my illusions, which no painter has ever been able to reproduce. Strange, isn't it, that no chemical will give a human being the iridescence that illusions give them? Give me your hat. You look so formal and uncomfortable! And so you finally tracked down my impersonations! But are you aware of the courage, the audacity which my profession requires? Very few people are gifted for it. I had the vocation. It showed very early in my capacity for deluding myself. I was one who could call a backyard a garden, a tenement apartment a house, and if I were late when I came home to avoid a scolding I could imagine and recreate instantly such interesting obstacles, adventures, that it would take my parents several minutes before they could shake off the spell and return to reality. I could step out of my ordinary self or my ordinary life into multiple selves and lives without attracting attention. I mean that my first crime as you may be surprised to hear, was committed against myself. I was then a corrupter of minors, and this minor was myself. What I corrupted was what is called the truth in favor of a more marvellous world. I could always improve on the facts. I was never arrested for this: it concerned only myself. My parents were not wise enough to see that such prestigitation of facts might pro-

*duce a great artist, or at least a great actress. They beat
me, to shake out the dust of delusions. But strangely
enough, the more my father beat me, the more abundant-
ly did this dust gather again, and it was not gray or brown
dust as you find it in its daily form, but what is known
to adventurers as fool's gold. Give me your coat. As an
investigator you may be more interested to know that in
self defense, I accuse the writers of fairytales. Not hunger,
not cruelty, not my parents, but these tales which promised that sleeping in the snow never caused pneumonia,
that bread never turned stale, that trees blossomed out
of season, that dragons could be killed with courage, that
intense wishing would be followed immediately by fulfillment of the wish. Intrepid wishing, said the fairytales,
was more effective than labor. The smoke issuing from
Aladdin's lamp was my first smokescreen, and the lies
learned from fairytales were my first perjuries. Let us say
I had perverted tendencies: I believed everything I read.*

Sabina laughed at her own words. Djuna thought she
was drinking too much and looked at her.

"What made you laugh, Sabina?"

"Meet the lie detector, Djuna. He may arrest me."

"Oh, Sabina. You've never done anything to be arrested
for!"

Djuna gazed at Sabina's face. The intentness of it, the
feverishness she had always seen on it was no longer that of
burning aliveness. There was a tightness to the features,
and fear in the eyes.

"I have to talk to you, Djuna . . . I can't sleep . . ."

"I tried to find you when I came from Paris. You
change your address so often, and even your name."

"You know I've always wanted to break the moulds which life forms around one if one lets them."

"Why?"

"I want to trespass boundaries, erase all identifications, anything which fixes one permanently into one mould, one place without hope of change."

"This is the opposite of what everyone usually wants, isn't it?"

"Yes, I used to say that I had housing problems: mine was that I didn't want a house. I wanted a boat, a trailer, anything that moved freely. I feel safest of all when no one knows where I am, when for instance, I'm in a hotel room where even the number is scratched off the door."

"But safe from what?"

"I don't know what I'm saving from detection, except perhaps that I'm guilty of several loves, of many loves instead of one."

"That's no crime. Merely a case of divided loves!"

"But the lies, the lies I have to tell . . . You know, just as some criminals tell you: 'I never found a way to get what I wanted except by robbery,' I often feel like saying: 'I have never found a way to get what I wanted except by lies'."

"Are you ashamed of it?"

Sabina grew frightened again. "There comes a moment with each man, in each relationship, when I feel lonely."

"Because of the lies?"

"But if I told the truth I would be not only lonely but also alone, and I would cause each one great harm. How can I tell Alan that for me he is like a father."

"That's why you deserted him over and over again, as

one must desert the parent, it's a law of maturity."

"You seem to exonerate me."

"I'm only exonerating you in relationship to Alan, in which you acted like a child."

"He is the only one I trust, the only one whose love is infinite, tireless, all-forgiving."

"That's not a man's love you are describing, and not even a father's love. It's a fantasy-father, an idealized father once invented by a needy child. This love you need, Alan has given you. In this form of love you are right to trust him. But you will lose him one day, for there are other Alans exactly as there are other Sabinas, and they too demand to live and to be matched. The enemy of a love is never outside, it's not a man or woman, it's what we lack in ourselves."

Sabina's head had fallen on her chest in a pose of contrition.

"You don't believe that this man is here to arrest me?"

"No, Sabina, that is what you imagine. It is your own guilt which you have endowed this man with. You probably see this guilt mirrored in every policeman, every judge, every parent, every personage with authority. You see it with other's eyes. It's a reflection of what you feel. It's your interpretation: the eyes of the world on your acts."

Sabina raised her head. Such a flood of memories submerged her and hurt her so deeply she was left without breath. She felt such pain. It was like the pain of the "bends" felt by deep sea divers when they came to the surface too quickly.

"In your fabricated world, Sabina, men were either

crusaders who would fight your battles for you, or judges continuing your parent's duties, or princes who had not yet come of age, and therefore could not be husbands."

"Free me," said Sabina to the lie detector. "Set me free. I've said that to so many men: 'Are you going to set me free?' " She laughed. "I was all ready to say it to you."

"You have to set yourself free. That will come with love . . ." said the lie detector.

"Oh, I've loved enough, if that could save one. I've loved plenty. Look at your note book. I'm sure it is full of addresses."

"You haven't loved yet," he said. "You've only been trying to love, beginning to love. Trust alone is not love, desire alone is not love, illusion is not love, dreaming is not love. All these were paths leading you out of yourself, it is true, and so you thought they led to another, but you never reached the other. You were only on the way. Could you go out now and find the other faces of Alan, which you never struggled to see, or accept? Would you find the other face of Mambo which he so delicately hid from you? Would you struggle to find the other face of Philip?"

"Is it my fault if they only turned *one* of their faces towards me?"

"You're a danger to other human beings. First of all you dress them in the costume of the myth: poor Philip, he is Siegfried, he must always sing in tune, and be everlastingly handsome. Do you know where he is now? In a hospital with a broken ankle. Due to immobility he has gained a great deal of weight. You turn your face away, Sabina? That was not the myth you made love to, is it?

If Mambo stopped drumming to go home and nurse his sick mother, would you go with him and boil injection needles? Would you, if another woman loved Alan, would you relinquish your child's claims upon his protectiveness? Will you go and make of yourself a competent actress and not continue to play Cinderella for amateur theatres only, keeping the artificial snow drop which fell on your nose during the snow storm long after the play is over as if to say: 'For me there is no difference at all between stage snow and the one falling now over Fifth Avenue?' Oh, Sabina, how you juggled the facts in your games of desire, so that you might always win. The one intent on winning has not loved yet!"

To the lie detector Sabina said: "And if I did all you ask of me, will you stop haunting my steps, will you stop writing in your note book?"

"Yes, Sabina. I promise you," he said.

"But, how could you know so much about my life . . ."

"You forget that you invited me yourself to shadow you. You endowed me with the power to judge your acts. You have endowed so many people with this power: priest, policemen, doctors. Shadowed by your conscience, interchangeable, you felt safer. You felt you could keep your sanity. Half of you wanted to atone, to be freed of the torments of guilt, but the other half wanted to be free. Only half of you surrendered, calling out to strangers: 'Catch me!' while the other half sought industriously to escape final capture. It was just another one of your flirtations, a flirtation with justice. And now you are in flight, from the guilt of love divided, and from the guilt of not loving. Poor Sabina, there was not enough to go

137

around. You sought your wholeness in music . . . Yours is a story of non-love . . . And do you know Sabina, if you had been caught and tried, you would have been meted out a less severe punishment than you mete out to yourself. We are much more severe judges of our own acts. We judge our thoughts, our secret intents, our dreams even . . . You never considered the mitigating circumstances. Some shock shattered you and made you distrustful of a single love. You divided them as a measure of safety. So many trap doors opened between the night club world of Mambo, to the Vienna-before-the-war of Philip, to the studious world of Alan, or the adolescent evanescent world of Donald. Mobility in love became a condition for your existence. There is nothing shameful in seeking safety measures. Your fear was very great."

"My trap doors failed me."

"Come with me, Sabina."

Sabina and Djuna went up to her studio, where they could still hear the drumming.

As if to silence it, Djuna placed a record in her phonograph.

"Sabina . . ." But no words came as one of Beethoven's Quartets began to tell Sabina as Djuna could not, of what they both knew for absolute certainty: the continuity of existence and of the chain of summits, of elevations by which such continuity is reached. By elevation the consciousness reached a perpetual movement, transcending death, and in the same manner attained the continuity of love by seizing upon its impersonal essence, which was a summation of all the alchemies producing life and birth, a child, a work of art, a work of science, a heroic act, an act of love. The identity of the human couple was not eternal but interchangeable, to protect this exchange of spirits, transmissions of character, all the fecundations of new selves being born, and faithfulness only to the continuity the extensions and expansions of love achieving their crystallizations into high moments and summits equal to the high moments and summits of art or religion.

Sabina slid to the floor and sat there with her head against the phonograph, with her wide skirt floating for one instant like an expiring parachute; and then deflated completely and died in the dust.

The tears on Sabina's face were not round and separate like ordinary tears, but seemed to have fallen like a water veil, as if she had sunk to the bottom of the sea by the weight and dissolutions of the music. There was a complete dissolution of the eyes, features, as if she were losing her essence.

The lie detector held out his hands as if to rescue her, in a light gesture, as if this were a graceful dance of sorrow rather than the sorrow itself, and said: "In homeopathy there is a remedy called pulsatile for those who weep at music."